"Amelia, I see you're dressed for outdoor work, so you go with Chase, and..."

Stunned by this turn of events, Amelia didn't hear the rest of Rick's assignments. She could *not* spend the day alone with Chase!

When Chase appeared at her side, saying quietly, "This will be like old times," Amelia knew it was too late to refuse politely. Were her steps destined to travel a path that would disrupt the even current of life she'd developed in the post-Chase era, as she always thought of the last fifteen years?

The eagerness in Chase's clear gray eyes was disconcerting, and she forced herself to regard him dispassionately, as she might look at a stranger. Amelia considered the man facing her *to be* a stranger. Very little that she'd noted in the short time they'd spent together yesterday had reminded her of the man who'd loved her, married her and disillusioned her so thoroughly that she had no interest in marrying again.

Books by Irene Brand

Love Inspired

Child of Her Heart #19
Heiress #37
To Love and Honor #49
*A Groom To Come
   Home To* #70
Tender Love #95
The Test of Love #114

Autumn's Awakening #129
Summer's Promise #148
*Love at Last #190
*Song of Her Heart #200
*The Christmas Children #234
*Second Chance at Love #244

*The Mellow Years

IRENE BRAND

Writing has been a lifelong interest of this author, who says that she started her first novel when she was eleven years old and hasn't finished it yet. However, since 1984, she's published thirty-two contemporary and historical novels and three nonfiction titles. She started writing professionally in 1977, after she completed her master's degree in history at Marshall University. Irene taught in secondary public schools for twenty-three years, but retired in 1989 to devote herself to writing.

Consistent involvement in the activities of her local church has been a source of inspiration for Irene's work. Traveling with her husband, Rod, to all fifty states and to thirty-two foreign countries has also inspired her writing. Irene is grateful to the many readers who have written to say that her inspiring stories and compelling portrayals of characters with strong faith have made a positive impression on their lives. You can write to her at P.O. Box 2770, Southside, WV 25187 or visit her Web site at www.irenebrand.com.

SECOND CHANCE
AT LOVE

IRENE BRAND

Love Inspired

Published by Steeple Hill Books™

STEEPLE HILL BOOKS

Steeple
Hill®

ISBN 0-373-87254-2

SECOND CHANCE AT LOVE

Visit us at www.steeplehill.com

Printed in U.S.A.

For He shall give His angels charge over thee,
to keep thee in all thy ways.
—*Psalms* 91:11

With appreciation to:

Bill Davis, County Emergency Director,
Mingo County, West Virginia;
Cecil E. Hatfield, Executive Director,
Tug Valley Chamber of Commerce;
Judy & Tom Ashley, Red Cross volunteers,
Putnam County, West Virginia;
Charlie Erwin, Office Coordinator, Red Cross,
Putnam County, West Virginia.

Chapter One

Amelia Stone didn't consider herself an impetuous woman until she said, "I want to go and help. Can you manage without me for three weeks?" Many times during the following few days, she questioned this comment to her supervisor.

After her usual morning routine, when Amelia had entered the American Red Cross office, she'd greeted Tom Matney, her supervisor, picked up a cup of coffee and gone to her computer to check the local and national news.

"Six dead, ten missing in flood," she'd read aloud.

"Where?" Tom asked.

"In southern West Virginia."

Amelia continued reading the computer message. "Several areas have been inundated with floodwaters from the Tug Fork River, a border stream between West Virginia and Kentucky.''

Before Amelia had finished reading the account of death and destruction, Tom laid a fax sheet on her desk—a call for help from the West Virginia Red Cross. She experienced an overwhelming urge to answer that call. Amelia wasn't naturally impulsive, so her reaction to this emergency surprised her, as well as her supervisor.

Tom had stared at her with incredulous eyes when she volunteered. A fourteen-year employee of the American Red Cross, Amelia had been exposed to many national tragedies, but she'd always been content to remain at her desk to do her part in helping the unfortunate.

"We're very busy, as you know," Tom said slowly, "but we must send help. Speed is of the essence in a calamity like this. If you can get ready to go today, I'll round up other volunteers to follow you as soon as possible."

The sudden devastation that had wrecked almost five thousand homes was enough to stir anyone's sympathy, and Amelia had felt a wave of compassion that she'd never known before. She was a warmhearted person, but never until this moment had she felt the need to physically help others.

By midafternoon, Amelia had left Philadelphia and was on her way to West Virginia. After her sudden decision, she'd made arrangements for a volunteer worker to take over her office duties. She'd gone to her apartment, packed her car with everything she thought she would need for three weeks and headed south in her Buick, a Christmas gift from her parents. Only then had she taken time to consider her hasty action.

Having been pampered by rich parents for years, Amelia decided in her late twenties to seek a more worthwhile life than the one she'd had up to that time. She'd gained a new social perspective when she became a Christian, and a sense of mission had led Amelia to work for the Red Cross. She knew she'd been of service as an office worker, so why did she have this sudden urge, at the mellow age of forty-three, to become personally involved?

Last night, during her devotional time, Amelia had read the apostle Paul's experience in the first century when he'd received a call to take the Gospel into Macedonia. "After Paul had seen the vision, we got ready at once to leave for Macedonia, concluding that God had called us to preach the Gospel to them."

Paul's experience fresh in her mind may have been the reason she'd responded so readily to the plight of the flood victims. But, to Amelia, it seemed more than that—it felt as if she'd had no control over the decision she'd made. As if there was no option at all—that God was directing her life in a way He had never done before.

"Why, God?" Amelia asked more than once as she traveled. When she reached Charleston, West Virginia, the next day, she still didn't have an answer.

She was welcomed heartily by the representatives at the Red Cross office on Virginia Street. The secretary informed Amelia she couldn't drive into the flood-ravaged area.

"Traffic is at a standstill in that part of the state," the woman said. "Roads and bridges have been destroyed, and many communities are completely isolated by the floodwaters. The National Guard is sending helicopters to rescue stranded people. The next flight goes in an hour, and they're taking a few volunteers. There's room for you. Take only absolute necessities. As soon as the water recedes, you can come back for your car."

Amelia wasn't thrilled about a helicopter ride, but she accepted it as readily as if she flew to work every day. She gathered a few changes of clothing and her toiletries, dumped them in a duffel bag and headed for the airport, where she parked her car and boarded the waiting helicopter.

The mountainous region didn't have enough flat land for an airport, and Yeager Airport was located on a wide expanse that had been formed by leveling several mountain peaks and filling in the valleys. The noise from the helicopter's whirling blades discouraged talking with the ten other volunteers on board, so Amelia focused her attention on the scenery. She looked with interest at the tugboat traveling northward on the big river that divided the city of Charleston. The golden dome of the state's Capitol gleamed in the midday sunlight.

The city was soon lost to view and the terrain became more rugged. Wooded mountain areas were bisected by narrow valleys, and to Amelia, who'd always lived in large cities, the scenery was breath taking. At the higher altitudes, the trees were leafless, but dogwood and redbud trees decorated the landscape with a mist of white and fuchsia blossoms. Numerous towns had been built along the banks of mountain streams. Frequently, the barrenness of strip mines marred her enjoyment of the scenery.

As they approached the flooded area, Amelia noticed that the mountains had been timbered. Discarded branches, left behind after logging, had blocked many streams. The absence of vegetation had no doubt contributed to a swift runoff of melted snow and heavy rains.

Amelia couldn't believe the havoc she saw when she looked down upon the flooded area as the helicopter neared the town of Williamson. The major business district was protected by a floodwall, but in the outlying districts, uprooted trees were coated with layers of mud and trash. Roads were washed away. Piles of rubble filled entire hollows where neighborhoods had once stood. Only the tops of automobiles and trucks protruded from the muddy water.

The helicopter landed on the pad at Williamson Memorial Hospital where a van waited to take them to Red Cross headquarters at Mountainview Church. As they rode toward the church in the van, Amelia sat beside a young woman, who was probably still in her teens.

"Hi, I'm Vicky Lanham," the girl said. "I live in Ohio, near Columbus. Our church keeps a semi-trailer outfitted for emergencies like this. Two of our members brought the truck to the area, but I took a plane into Charleston. I've never seen anything like the destruction we saw from the 'copter."

"I work for the American Red Cross in Philadelphia," Amelia answered. "I usually stay in the office and handle the paperwork, but I volunteered to come onsite, and here I am." She paused, wondering if her doubts were apparent to the young woman, but then continued. "I'm not sure what I've gotten myself into."

"It's gonna be a lot of hard work, but my parents prodded me into coming," Vicky said. "I think God is calling me to be a missionary, and Dad said that some primitive living and hard work here will be a good introduction to what I can expect on the mission field. Why did you volunteer?"

"I'm not sure," Amelia admitted. "I just had the

overwhelming belief that I should take this assignment.''

''Maybe God was pushing you, just like my parents prodded me.''

Amelia laughed. ''You might have a point there. It will be good for us to gain a new understanding of how God's work is accomplished on the raw side of life.''

The van labored up the steep incline and stopped before a sprawling, two-story stone church building. ''If this is our headquarters, life can't be *too* bad. By the way, my name is Amelia Stone, and I'm looking forward to working with you.''

The church was built on a mountain above the floodplain, and the Red Cross had opened a service center in the building. After the volunteers had introduced themselves, the director of Red Cross operations in the region—a tall, gangly man in his fifties—assigned Vicky and Amelia to jobs immediately.

''I'm Rick Smith,'' he said. ''And you're as welcome here as the flowers in May.'' To Vicky, he said, ''Your church's truck has arrived, even though the men had to take a roundabout route to get here. We'll start handing out the supplies they brought as soon as you get settled.''

''I have my laptop, so I can set up shop wherever you want me to,'' Amelia said.

''Good,'' Rick said. ''Let's go into the gymnasium. That's where the men from Ohio are unloading their supplies. Three dozen flood victims stayed here last night. You can start processing their applications for help right away.''

Vicky and Amelia preceded him into the crowded gym, and tears of compassion stung Amelia's eyes when she saw the bedraggled people staring at them. The elderly, the middle-aged and several children sat quietly in the room, no evidence of hope in their bleak eyes.

God, she prayed silently. *These people have lost everything except You. Be very near them today. Use me as Your instrument to bring peace to their hearts.*

Amelia sat at the folding table Rick Smith brought and started her computer. While she waited for her programs to appear on the screen, her fingers drummed idly on the table as she glanced around the large room. Two men were carrying buckets, mops, brooms, cartons of bottled water and cartons of cleaning supplies into the gym. Amelia surmised that they were the men from Vicky's church.

A quick breath of astonishment burst from Amelia's lips as she took a closer look at one of the men. Even his back looked familiar. He could be a Red Cross representative she'd met before, though she thought the recognition went beyond that.

As she watched, the man turned, and a shock of disbelief shattered her composure. Although his fair, wavy hair was silvering a bit at the temples, and the years had etched deeper lines on his face, there was no mistaking the classic features and clear gray eyes of Chase Ramsey. Imagine meeting him again after fifteen years!

Amelia's stomach knotted and she shuddered inwardly. She lowered her eyes, hoping Chase wouldn't recognize her.

God, I'm not ready for this. If Chase is the reason You brought me to West Virginia, I'm ready to go home now.

Amelia had thought she'd put the past behind her, but obviously, she needed more time to erase the grief Chase had caused her. And she was suddenly overcome with a sense of loss when she considered that, in all probability, Chase might be married.

Chase Ramsey straightened from placing a large carton of bottled water on the floor. He waved at Vicky, and his gaze rested on the woman beside her as he turned to bring in another load of supplies. He stopped in his tracks. Instantly aware of his scrutiny, Amelia looked up, and recognition dawned in his eyes. He walked quickly across the room.

"Of all places to meet you!" Chase said as he reached for Amelia's hand. The surprise in his eyes was replaced by pleasure as he admired Amelia. Still as beautiful as ever, he thought, wondering if he should have been more discreet. Remembering her harsh words at their last encounter, he realized that Amelia might not share his joy in this meeting.

Amelia was still a graceful woman, of medium height in her early forties. She held her well-formed body erect. Heavy brown hair surrounded her pale golden skin, and she looked at him with enormous dark eyes. Her lips parted in a slight smile, but the smile didn't reach her eyes. Amelia had always worn expensive clothes, and Chase thought she looked like a harbinger of spring in her sea-green pants suit and floral print blouse.

Amelia placed her hand in his, saying calmly, "Hello, Chase." She hoped he wasn't aware of the anxiety and frustration churning in her stomach.

Rick Smith and Vicky watched this reunion, and Rick said, "Apparently you've met before."

"Guess you could say that," Chase said, grinning broadly. "Have you been introduced? Rick, this is Amelia…" He paused, and looked questioningly at Amelia's left hand.

"It's still Stone," she said with an unreadable expression.

"Well, a lot could have happened since I've seen you, so I didn't know."

"I've already met Rick, and Vicky, too," she said.

"Do you live in this area, Amelia?"

Conscious that Chase still held her hand, she pulled it from his grasp. "No, I'm here as a volunteer to help the flood victims. I came in a National Guard helicopter a short time ago."

"And we have to get to work," Rick said, fidgeting from one foot to another.

"Sorry," Chase apologized. "We can talk this evening, Amelia. It's good to see you again."

Amelia looked after Chase as he returned to work. The knit shirt and well-worn jeans he wore enhanced his muscular physique. Chase was slightly taller than she was, and his compact, lean body moved with easy grace. Physically, he had changed very little since the last time they'd seen each other.

"I'm surprised that you know Mr. Ramsey," Vicky said at her elbow.

"What?" Amelia had forgotten about the girl. "Oh, yes, we were in college together. How'd you know him?"

"He's one of the men who came from our church with the truck full of supplies."

Chase, a church member? What a surprise! When Amelia had known him, he wouldn't have been found inside a church. And neither would I, she thought with a wry smile. She wanted to question Vicky about Chase, but people were queuing up in front of her, so Amelia turned her attention to helping them.

The afternoon's activities allowed no time for reflection as she screened and approved applications from people whose homes had been destroyed by water or mud slides. Those who needed medication got attention first, and when Chase finished unloading the truck, he used the church van to drive several people to another town where, with Red Cross vouchers, they could buy their medicine.

When the center closed at six-thirty, Amelia stood, wearily stretching her back muscles and flexing her fingers. Delicious odors wafted from the church's kitchen, and Amelia realized that she hadn't eaten since breakfast. The pastor of the church, Allen Chambers, approached Vicky and Amelia.

"We're housing flood victims in the gym, but we have temporary facilities for you and the male workers on the second floor. Bring your luggage, and I'll show you to your quarters so you can freshen up a bit before we eat."

As Amelia and Vicky followed Allen Chambers upstairs, he explained, "We have a day school here at the church, but classes have been canceled during this crisis. We're fortunate to have enough space to provide a service center."

He opened a door into the primary department. "There are rest room facilities in here, a bit small for you, but I thought we should leave the larger rooms next door for the men. More workers will be here tomorrow, but you won't be crowded tonight." Grinning, Allen Chambers pointed to a stack of cots and bed linens.

"We don't have maid service, so you'll have to fix your own beds."

Amelia had grown up with maid service, but after she started making her own living, she couldn't afford to pay anyone to clean for her. A long roll of thunder reverberated around the building and gusts of rain struck the windows.

"It's raining *again!*" Vicky cried. "What *are* these people going to do?"

"It is bad," the pastor said. "And the worst part, many of these victims had their homes destroyed less than a year ago. This is the second time in a few months they've been left homeless. Well, anyway, I'll see you at dinnertime," Allen Chambers said, and closed the door after him.

"He's cute, isn't he?" Vicky said.

"He's very handsome," Amelia agreed, but at Vicky's next comment, she knew they weren't thinking about the same man.

"He seems kind of young to be the pastor of a big church like this."

A brawny man, Allen Chambers's strong face was marked by freckles. His light blue eyes were deep-set in his face, and he had an outgoing personality. Cute? Perhaps he was, Amelia thought, but when compared to Chase's lean body, Chambers's bulk seemed overwhelming to her.

Amelia took a quick wash in a lavatory whose facilities weren't higher than her knees, and after

Vicky took her turn, they spread sheets and blankets on their cots while Vicky chattered about the unfortunate flood victims. Amelia tried to give the correct responses to her companion's comments, but her thoughts were in the past.

She'd met Chase when she was a junior in college. He was the most popular man on campus. He'd dated a lot of women, so she had a lot of competition and considered herself fortunate when he'd focused his exclusive attention on her. Now he was back in her life after fifteen years. Was she pleased or sorry to see him again?

Amelia had no answer for that question. She'd changed a lot, and probably Chase had, too. Her reaction to meeting him today had been annoyance more than anything else. She was getting along fine as she was—she no longer had any desire for masculine companionship. She and Chase had enjoyed being together, and were compatible in many ways. Yet something had always seemed to be missing, something to make their happiness complete. When she'd accepted the Lord into her life, she knew immediately what they'd lacked to have a satisfying relationship.

According to Vicky, Chase was active in his church, so he'd had a change of heart, too. Would this mutual interest make a difference in any future encounters they might share?

Chapter Two

Amelia knew she couldn't put Chase off if he wanted to talk to her, but she was relieved that they didn't have time to visit during dinner. The volunteer staff mingled with the flood victims, and Chase and she didn't have an opportunity to speak in the dining room. Her thoughts were diverted from him as she listened to the heartbreaking stories the victims told of their narrow escapes from the floodwaters.

She sat across the table from an elderly couple, Josh and Mandy Newberry, who seemed bewildered by what had happened.

"We've lived in that holler for most of our lives," Josh said in a deep voice. "And this is the first time we've ever been flooded out. There have been little floods, but nothing like this one."

"Everything we've saved all those years is gone," Mandy said in a quavering voice, tears in her eyes. "If I'd just had time to save the pictures of my young'uns! All my memories are gone, too."

Josh patted her hand. "No, Mandy. Your memories ain't gone. And we'll make out all right. We've got the good Lord on our side. He's seen us through a lot of other trouble, and He'll see us through this'n."

Amelia's throat tightened in compassion, but she smiled at the Newberrys. "That's right. One of my favorite Scriptures is 'I was young and now I am old, yet I have never seen the righteous forsaken or their children begging bread.' God will provide for you, and He's sent me and many other people to help you." She gripped each of their right hands. "Try to get a good night's sleep. Maybe the sun will shine tomorrow."

"God bless you, young lady," Mandy said. "You've already perked me up."

Amelia left the dining room to go upstairs to her quarters, seeking some privacy. She was surprised, and annoyed, at the emotional turmoil she was experiencing because she'd encountered Chase again. She'd voluntarily walked away from him fifteen years ago without a backward glance, and as the years passed, often weeks would go by when she didn't think about him. So why had Chase's surprise appearance sent her pulses spinning? Why was she filled with unease at being around him in this cleanup effort?

Chase had been visiting with Allen Chambers when Amelia left the gym, and she'd hoped to escape talking to him tonight. Instead of going to the cubbyhole she'd be sharing with Vicky, Amelia followed the signs to the chapel, a small room with an altar, a lectern, a few pews and an illuminated cross in the background that dimly lit the room. She knelt by the altar to pray, but words were hard to find. She did pray for the flood victims, asking for strength and wisdom to make a difference in their lives. Since she didn't know how to pray about Chase, she simply asked for guidance in every aspect of her life during these weeks she'd be spending in the mountains.

When she rose from her knees, Amelia had the sensation that she wasn't alone. She turned quickly.

Chase leaned gracefully against the doorframe. His stunning good looks captured her attention as if she was seeing him for the first time. He'd changed from the shorts he'd worn earlier. His tailored brown slacks revealed a lean, sinewy, youthful body. His waist and hips were thin, but his broad shoulders stretched the fabric of his brightly colored shirt, which emphasized the gold flecks in his gray eyes. Chase had always looked well put together, like a male model.

"I didn't mean to startle you," he apologized.

"Maybe this is a good place for us to talk?" He spoke hesitantly, as if he doubted his welcome.

Amelia's head swirled with doubts, and she experienced momentary panic, but she didn't want him to know her feelings. "Why not? It's quiet here," she said calmly.

"Looks like a good place to me," he agreed.

They sat on the front pew, not close, but in comfortable conversing distance. Several minutes passed in tense silence, each of them waiting for the other to speak. What could they say to bridge fifteen years?

"The Amelia Stone I knew wouldn't be praying in a chapel," Chase said at last. In the dim light, his gray eyes seemed dark and unfathomable.

"Thanks to God, *that* Amelia Stone is gone." She seemed to be in a Scripture-quoting mood today, Amelia thought humorously as she continued. "'If anyone is in Christ, he is a new creation, the old has gone, the new has come!' Vicky tells me that you're a member of her church, so you're probably familiar with that verse."

"Yes. It's true for me, too. I've been a Christian for several years."

"Then neither of us is the person we used to be, which is for the best, I think."

"What are you doing now, Amelia? I never meant to lose track of you, but the years passed quickly."

"I'd had enough of being a rich man's kid, so I

left home to make it on my own. I wanted a job that would make a difference in other people's lives, so I went to work for the Red Cross in Philadelphia. I've been there for several years. My parents never did have much time for me, so I'm pretty much on my own.'' She scanned his face briefly. ''Now it's your turn.''

''I'm working at a bank in Worthington, Ohio. I transferred there from Chicago twelve years ago.''

She took a deep breath and plunged into chancy territory. ''I assume you're married?''

''No, I haven't married.''

A tremor touched her lips and, hoping he hadn't noticed, she changed the subject. ''How long are you going to be here in Mingo County?'' Amelia asked.

He paused thoughtfully, before he answered. ''I'd only intended to unload our truck and go back home, but if I can arrange to take some of my vacation now, I might stay for a few weeks. I didn't realize the extent of the disaster until I got here.''

''Neither did I. I want to help as much as possible, and I need some rest. It's been a long day.''

Uncomfortable with the knowledge that Chase might extend his stay, Amelia stood and headed toward the door. She'd be more comfortable emotionally if he went back to Ohio. Was he really concerned about the flood victims, or was he staying because of her?

Chase walked alongside her to the door of her sleeping quarters. "My buddy and I are in the room next door," he said. "If you need anything, pound on the wall, and I'll hear you."

"Thanks. See you in the morning."

Chase walked into his room, thankful that his friend from the church was already sleeping. He undressed quietly, turned off the light and lay on the cot, wide-eyed. He'd been awake for almost twenty-four hours. He should be ready to sleep, but he couldn't stop thinking about Amelia. Memories of the past plagued his mind. He remembered much about their time together—memories he'd be better off forgetting. Seeing what Amelia had become, he realized anew what a *big* mistake he'd made when he'd let her slip out of his life.

He stirred uneasily on the cot, a very uncomfortable place to sleep, but that wasn't the cause of his distress. His marriage to Amelia had lasted for almost five years, and he kept remembering the intimate moments they'd shared. He was even more restless when he remembered the reason for their divorce, and who was to blame.

Amelia awakened sluggishly, her befuddled mind hazily questioning why she was sleeping on a board instead of her comfortable mattress. She stretched, turned over and barely missed tumbling off the narrow cot onto the floor. Her eyes popped open as reality surfaced. She was in a disaster area of West Virginia, not her Philadelphia apartment.

Cloud-darkened daylight crept into the schoolroom where she slept in the company of Vicky, who had abandoned her narrow bed and was curled up, kittenlike, on the floor with a yellow blanket wrapped around her. Rubbing the crick in her neck and her aching back muscles, Amelia thought the floor might have been preferable to the cot.

Amelia stifled her moment of self-pity, remembering that many people on the first floor of the building not only didn't have a comfortable bed, but no home to put one in. Moving quietly so she wouldn't disturb Vicky, Amelia stood, stretched her stiff muscles and went to the bathroom. Allen Chambers had mentioned last night that there was a shower room adjacent to the gymnasium, but Amelia knew the disaster victims would need that facility. She took a skimpy sponge bath with water from the lavatory.

She dressed in heavy socks, jeans, a pullover sweater and the knee-high waterproof boots her supervisor had insisted that she must have. Even though it was late April, this mountainous area was cold.

Pastor Chambers had mentioned that the church women would be serving breakfast at seven o'clock. When Amelia finished dressing, it was half-past six. She called Vicky's name quietly, and the girl awakened immediately, seemingly none the worse for sleeping on the floor all night. Youth! Amelia thought enviously, when she compared the young woman's bright and cheery attitude to her own low spirits. She doubted, though, that the uncomfortable cot was the only cause of her wretchedness this morning.

Amelia was usually more peppy upon awakening, and she knew that her exhaustion resulted from mental—rather than physical—fatigue. She hadn't rested physically, because an overburdened mind had contributed to her restless night. Why had running into Chase caused her so much misery? She'd occasionally wondered how seeing him again would affect her. She'd never expected to experience the devastating anguish that had seared her heart the moment she had seen her ex-husband yesterday.

Memories of the past smothered Amelia, and she called to Vicky, who was still in the bathroom. "I'm going out for some fresh air. I'll meet you in the gym."

Leaving by the front door of the church, Amelia walked to the crest of the hill and looked out over the river valley. Below her, a two-lane highway, far above the river, provided some transportation. No trains moved along the railroad track at the base of the mountain, because the tracks were blocked by a floodwall gate. The Tug Fork River, the border between West Virginia and Kentucky, lapped several feet on the wall that protected the town of Williamson.

Remembering the devastation she'd seen from the helicopter, Amelia's faith faltered momentarily. Why did God allow such destruction? She considered the apostle Paul and the many terrible things that happened to him. His faith had remained steadfast during all of his trials. Why bad things happen to good people was a question she'd never been able to answer.

Amelia hadn't volunteered for this mission to ask questions. She was here to help troubled people, and she had to put aside her spiritual doubts and personal turmoil. Wondering what her duties would be today, Amelia turned back toward the church, praying that God would use her to make a difference in the lives of the flood victims.

After breakfast, Rick Smith stood on a small platform and called for their attention.

"I want to thank all of you volunteers for your prompt response to our needs. I've lived in this area all of my life, and I'll quickly give you a brief rundown on our history. The first settlers arrived in the late eighteenth century, but the town of Williamson was organized a hundred years later. The heyday of our town was during the early twentieth century. Our population today is about five thousand, half of what it was a century ago. Many of our historic buildings were destroyed by frequent floods before we had floodwall protection, and many were razed to make room for the floodwall. Although it's not what it used to be, Williamson is still a good place to live, and I hope you'll feel welcome in the area.

"Today's most urgent need is to find out how many people need help and to provide as much comfort as possible until more volunteers and supplies arrive.

"As soon as the roads are passable, several out-of-state churches will send portable kitchens and a staff to operate them," he said. "They'll do the cooking in a few central places, and our volunteers will take the food to the disaster areas. Today we need to canvas all of the flooded areas we can reach, see what the needs are and help as many people as we can. We can't provide hot food today, but Chase and his buddy brought a lot of canned juice, water and snacks."

"How long will it be before we can reach all the flooded areas?" a volunteer asked.

"The floodwaters are receding now, but representatives of the U.S. Corps of Engineers say that it will be weeks before we can drive into all of the affected areas. A lot of infrastructure has been destroyed. Go today prepared to hike into areas where the roads are impassable."

"When will more Red Cross volunteers arrive?" someone in the crowd asked.

Rick Smith shook his head. "I don't know. The National Guard brought in a few, but their helicopters are busy rescuing stranded people now. There are several truckloads of supplies stalled at the highway rest stop near Beckley, waiting to be delivered. As soon as the roads are open, we'll have hundreds of helpers. It will be several days before we can get all of our supplies, emergency vehicles and more volunteers. In the meantime, we'll make do with what we have. Today, I'm assigning you in teams of two to go out and assess the needs and help where possible."

Rick Smith answered several questions from the flood victims, who wanted to know when they could go home. Over five inches of rain had fallen on the area in a twelve-hour period, and many people had escaped the rapidly rising water with nothing more than the clothes they were wearing. Understandably, they were anxious about the possessions, pets and neighbors they'd had to leave behind.

After he compassionately explained that it might be days before the people could leave this temporary shelter, Rick Smith asked, "Have any of you volunteers ever driven a Jeep?"

Amelia hadn't seen Chase all morning, and she was startled when his voice sounded close behind her.

"I did, during my four-year stint in the army. I probably haven't forgotten how."

Amelia was surprised to learn that Chase had been in the army. That had apparently happened after they'd broken up.

Another man indicated that he'd once owned a Jeep, and Rick Smith said, "Good. We've borrowed a couple of Jeeps from the National Guard until we can get our rental vehicles, so you guys can drive them and scout out some of the isolated hollows today." His gaze scanned the few volunteers.

"Amelia, I see you're dressed for outdoor work, so you go with Chase, and…"

Stunned by this turn of events, Amelia didn't hear the rest of the assignments. She could *not* spend the day alone with Chase! Her erratic heartbeat almost took her breath away, and she became more uncomfortable as her dismay increased.

Rick had moved on with the daily plans, not giving Amelia the opportunity to accept or reject the assignment.

When Chase appeared at her side, saying quietly, "This will be like old times," Amelia knew it was too late to politely refuse. Were her steps destined to travel a path that would disrupt the even current of life she'd developed in the post-Chase era, as she always thought of the last fifteen years?

The eagerness in Chase's clear gray eyes was disconcerting, and she forced herself to regard him dispassionately, as she might look at a stranger. Amelia considered the man facing her *was* a stranger. Very little that she'd noted in the short time they'd spent together yesterday had reminded her of the man who'd loved her, married her and disillusioned her so thoroughly that she had no interest in marrying again.

Chapter Three

Amelia decided to accept the inevitable. She wouldn't be able to avoid contact with Chase, but she was determined to prevent him from hurting her again.

"While you load provisions in the Jeep, I'll bring my laptop," she said, praying that her casual tone would convince Chase that he was no more to her than a business acquaintance. *Which was true, wasn't it?* "I can use the computer to record our findings," she added.

Amelia went to her makeshift bedroom for the laptop and a hooded plastic parka, because more rain was predicted today. She filled a tote bag with personal items she might need.

Seated in a camouflaged Jeep, Chase waited in front of the church, and he handed her a white Disaster Relief vest with a red band around the bottom and a large red cross on the back. "We have to wear these all the time when we're out on a volunteer mission."

The Jeep didn't have any doors, just a fabric roof, so Amelia climbed in beside Chase and adjusted the seat belt. She removed a woolen cloche from her tote and put it on her head. She pitched the tote into the back seat, opened her laptop, steadying it on her knees.

"Let's go," she said.

How could a man wearing a heavy woolen jacket, jeans, a pair of rubber boots and a hat covered with plastic appear attractive? On Chase, the work clothes lent an air of masculinity that enhanced his handsome features.

Thunder sounded in the distance and a few sprinkles accumulated on the windshield.

"It was a good idea to bring your parka. I have a raincoat on the back seat if I need it," he said.

Chase nosed the Jeep toward the edge of the mountain and down the steep incline toward the river valley. After driving a few miles eastward on the paved highway, he turned left on a narrow, rutted, muddy road, and shifted into four-wheel drive. Red clay mud flew in all directions as, with difficulty, he maneuvered the Jeep upward along the hazardous mountain terrain.

"Are you sure this is the right road?" Amelia said as she clutched the seat with both hands.

"I'm beginning to wonder. Rick Smith said to take the first road to the left, but this must not have been the one he meant." Glancing over his shoulder at the steep, crooked road, he said, "I can't go back now."

The road wound up and down and around the mountain, and within fifteen minutes, sweat dripped from Chase's forehead into his eyes. Knowing he didn't dare take his hands from the steering wheel, Amelia held on with one hand and took a handful of tissues from her pocket. She wiped the moisture from his face. Her fingers tingled when they brushed the day-old stubble of his whiskers, reminding her of the days when she'd awakened at his side, her smooth face resting against his scratchy one.

"Thanks," he said.

His words stuck in his throat as they entered a sharp dip and the front wheels of the Jeep dropped into a demolished culvert. The decline was so sudden that, in spite of her seat belt, Amelia's body bounced forward and her head hit the windshield.

"Ouch!" she said.

Struggling to pull the Jeep out of the gaping ditch, Chase couldn't spare her a glance, but he asked quickly, "Are you hurt?"

"Not much. Don't worry about me. Just get out of the ditch. I'd hate to be stranded up here."

In an attempt to control the twisting and turning vehicle as it writhed like a serpent in the sticky, reddish mud, Chase gunned the engine and gripped the steering wheel until his knuckles whitened. When he maneuvered the Jeep to level ground, Chase stopped and lowered his head on the wheel, his shoulders heaving as he struggled for breath.

"I don't know if I can take much more of this. I've never driven on such a road."

"Road? This isn't a road—it's a disaster!" Amelia took a small bottle of water from her tote. "Want a drink?"

"And how!" Chase said. He unscrewed the lid and gulped more than half of the water. "I don't know what to do now, but I guess we'll keep going forward—it couldn't be any worse than retracing our route."

"I shouldn't think so," Amelia agreed.

Shifting into gear, Chase said, "Talk to me while I drive. You're too quiet."

Torn by conflicting emotions, Amelia chose her words carefully. "This road has scared me silent, and I don't know what to say to you, anyway. Maybe you haven't been upset by our surprise reunion, but it's been awkward for me. I don't want to talk about the past, and this flood disaster isn't a pleasant subject."

"Then talk about your parents. How are they?"

"I don't see much of them. You know that

Mother and Dad had been married ten years when I was born, and they'd already molded their marriage without a child. When I went home after our divorce, Mother insisted that I move into my own apartment. I assumed that a divorced daughter was an embarrassment to them, that their friends would think they hadn't guided me correctly. Since I didn't think they'd want me living in the same town, I moved out of state. After Dad retired, they sold their holdings in Illinois and moved to Hilton Head permanently. I never did fit into their plans. I used to resent that, but I've gotten over it.''

As she continued, Chase wondered if she *had* come to terms with her parents' neglect.

''To make up for their lack of devotion, they offered to give me a generous monthly allowance to cover all my needs. They didn't like it when I got a job. I convinced them that I can make it on my own, but they still shower me with gifts. They bought a new Buick, which I didn't want, for Christmas. I make enough money to buy a car when I need one, but I was perfectly satisfied with my five-year-old Volkswagen.''

Her parents had liked Chase and, without knowing the circumstances, had blamed Amelia for the divorce. She'd remained silent, letting them believe what they wanted to. On the other hand, Chase's parents had always resented Amelia, and were pleased when he, in their words, ''got rid of her.''

In spite of his preoccupation with the difficult driving, Chase remembered that Amelia's parents had bought costly, and often inappropriate, gifts for her birthday and Christmas, but that hadn't compensated for the lack of their presence. After they'd spent thousands of dollars to give Amelia a lavish wedding, they seemed to think they'd done their duty by her. They occasionally stopped to see Amelia and Chase, but only for brief visits on their way to business conferences or frequent vacations. The Stones took a cruise each Christmas, and Amelia had spent few holidays with her parents after graduating from high school. And since his parents didn't like Amelia, Chase hadn't gone home for holidays, either, until after their divorce.

After a mile or two of torturous travel, the mountain road dipped into a hollow and joined a graveled road along a creek. Only a scant amount of water remained on the road, but the creek was still bankfull. Abandoned railroad tracks lay along the bank of the stream. Evidence of disaster was everywhere. The floodwaters had covered housetops, and rain-soaked curtains drooped drearily from open windows that had been broken by the swift current. Chain-link fences had been torn out by the deadly torrent, the metal twisted together and dumped in mutilated heaps beside the creek bed.

As they drove slowly upstream, Chase said worriedly, "I wonder if I took the wrong road. Rick said there was a town up this hollow."

"If so, the residents might have perished in the flood. Not many people could have survived this deluge," Amelia said.

They reached a spot where the strong water had stripped off the surface of the road, and Chase braked abruptly. For several yards, only two or three feet of roadbed separated two yawning ditches filled with pieces of pavement and foul-smelling water. A sharp curve blocked their view of what lay before them.

"Looks like the end of the road. I'll walk for a mile or so to see if I can find any survivors," Chase said.

Amelia unlocked her seat belt and stepped out of the vehicle into an inch of water on the roadbed.

"You don't have to go," Chase protested.

"This is a joint venture," she replied. "I'll do my part."

Shifting the Jeep into Reverse, Chase backed up cautiously until he found a place wide enough to turn the vehicle. Although it hadn't started raining yet, the clouds looked ominous, and he wanted to be headed out of this hollow if there was another cloudburst. He pocketed the keys, adjusted a heavy pack filled with food and first-aid supplies over his back. He hurried to join Amelia, who'd already crossed the narrow pathway and waited for him.

In places, they walked through water, and Amelia was thankful for her heavy boots. After they'd journeyed about a mile, Chase suggested that they turn around, but Amelia pointed to a spiral of smoke ahead of them. She was already tired from the unfamiliar exertion, but her steps quickened. She was both eager and fearful to learn the condition of the town's residents.

After rounding another bend in the road, they climbed a small hill and saw several buildings scattered haphazardly at the head of the hollow. Some houses had been washed off their foundations, outbuildings were now piles of shattered wood, tops of automobiles projected from the creek, a thick layer of black mud covered the ground, plastic bottles and other debris hung from tree branches. Chase pointed at a ramshackle mine shaft and tipple on the mountainside behind the houses.

"According to Rick Smith," he said, "this used to be a coal town, but the mine was abandoned several years ago. The coal company let the people buy their houses at a reasonable cost."

Amazingly, a debris-covered bridge still straddled the stream, but water lapped at the wooden floor. Chase tested the stability of the bridge by taking a few uncertain steps on the wet surface.

"Careful!" Amelia cautioned him, holding her breath.

"It's safe enough," Chase said, and he took Amelia's hand and held it tightly as they crossed the wobbly structure.

They sank ankle-deep into the black mud that sucked at their feet as they walked up the town's one street. Layers of mud and trash covered the ground. Cars were tangled in a net of mud and dead trees. Except for the swirling echoes of the still-swollen stream, a deadly silence greeted them. A few dwellings had collapsed under the force of the water, which had also forced doors and windows open on the remaining houses.

"Anybody home?" Chase called several times.

At first, the town seemed deserted, until they heard the faint sound of music. Momentarily, Amelia and Chase stared at one another in amazement, before they broke into a run, following the curve of the street. Disbelieving, they stopped in their tracks.

A two-story house had been torn in two by the energy of the water, and the lean-to rear section had toppled to the ground. The half-house seemed sturdy, smoke drifted upward from its chimney, and on the front porch, an elderly man sat in a rocking chair, eyes closed, strumming a banjo.

"Hello!" Chase said.

The man's eyes popped open, and his chin dropped several inches.

"Where on earth did you come from?" he said. Laying aside his banjo, and favoring his presumably arthritic knees, he clambered off the porch. The squat man, who looked as if he were in his eighties, grabbed Chase's hand.

"Young feller, I've never been so glad to see anyone in my life. You got any water? I ain't had a drink for three days."

Without waiting for Chase to remove the backpack, Amelia unzipped it, took out a bottle of water, uncapped it and handed it to the man. While the clear liquid gurgled down his throat, she unwrapped two granola bars and handed them to him. His hands were filthy, but he held the bars in the wrapper and ate them. The way he wolfed the food indicated that he probably hadn't eaten for three days, either.

He leaned against the porch and motioned toward the mine shaft. "An old sedimentation pond broke open and spilled gallons of slurry into our houses and polluted our wells. I've been afraid to eat or drink anything."

Amelia handed him some antibacterial hand wipes. While he cleaned his hands, she quickly peeled an orange and gave the sections to him.

He ate greedily, but between bites, he said, "'Scuse my manners, but hunger and thirst was about to get to me."

"What happened to all of your neighbors?" Chase asked.

He shook his head worriedly. "There's only twenty-five folks living here now. Some of them were gone when the flood struck, so I suppose they're staying with family. A few others took to the hills before the water surrounded their houses, and walked over the mountain to their kin. I watched the creek rise, and I stayed as long as I could. When it got to the edge of my yard, I grabbed my banjo and climbed the mountain. I stayed up there in an old lean-to until the water went down.''

''Why was the banjo more important to you than your other possessions?'' Amelia asked, wondering about his choice.

''This was my daddy's banjo,'' he said, patting the instrument fondly. ''I prize it more than anything else I have.''

''The Red Cross has a shelter set up not far from Williamson,'' Chase said. ''We have a Jeep parked down the road about a mile, and we can take you to the shelter.''

''No, thanks.''

''But, Mr....'' Chase paused. ''I guess we haven't been introduced. I'm Chase Ramsey, and this is Amelia Stone. We're working with the Red Cross to help flood victims.''

''My name's Willie Honaker. Call me Willie.''

''But, Willie, you shouldn't stay here,'' Amelia said. ''The road has washed away, and no vehicles can drive up the hollow to bring fuel or food for you.''

''I ain't leavin' my home. The forepart of the house is stable, and my fireplace is all right. The water didn't get upstairs, and I've got a bed up there. I aim to watch over my things and protect my neighbors' homes from thieves until they can come back. We ain't got much left, but I'm staying here.''

Amelia slanted an apprehensive look toward Chase. It would be a long time before the road would be passable for any of these residents to come home, let alone any thieves.

''There'll be government grants to help you to build, I'd imagine. In the meantime, you'd be more comfortable at the shelter,'' she insisted.

Willie resumed his seat in the chair, and slowly rocked back and forth, shaking his head negatively. ''Nope. I don't want government help. I've been lookin' after myself for a long time. If you've got any more water or candy bars, I'll make do until some of my kin come to look about me.''

Not knowing how many other needy people they'd encounter before the day was over, Chase gave Willie only half of the provisions he carried.

Before they left, Chase explained to Willie about the hazardous road they'd encountered. ''Is there an easier way to get back to Williamson?''

Willie's clear black eyes widened in astonishment.

''Man, you surely didn't take a road across the mountain!''

''Rick Smith said to take the first road to the left. That's what I did.''

"You must have been on a log road, made by contractors who've timbered that mountain. How'd you do it?"

With an embarrassed laugh, Chase said, "It wasn't easy."

"Young feller, I'd say you're a pretty good driver or you'd still be on top of the mountain. You just follow the road in the creek valley, and it'll take you to the highway."

Although he'd been in doubt about whether he should stay any longer in the disaster area, on the way back to the Jeep, Chase made up his mind. He received four weeks' vacation each year, and he'd take part of it to help here. He would get in touch with the bank to make arrangements if he could find a place to use his cell phone.

Would Amelia be pleased that he was staying? As they plodded through the thick mud, he told Amelia the decision he'd made. She nodded without saying anything, and he couldn't tell from her expression if she was annoyed, pleased or just didn't care what he did. He compared the Amelia he'd known to the woman with him today.

Because Amelia's mother had kept her in new clothes, and since she'd had an unlimited credit card, she'd set the fashion on campus. She'd bought anything that had caught her eye, and all clothes had looked good on her. Amelia hadn't been a snob, but because of her affluence, she'd outclassed most of the other students. She'd been a beautiful girl, and he'd wanted her the first time he'd seen her.

The roadbed was narrow in places, and Amelia walked in front of him, allowing ample opportunity for Chase to consider the person she'd become—a tall, willowy woman with a resolute mouth, candid dark eyes and long, very straight, brown hair that, today, fell in scraggly tufts over her shoulders. In her college days, she wouldn't have been caught dead looking as she did now. Soft rain had started, and they'd forgotten to bring their raincoats. Amelia's heavy sweater was soaked. Her jeans were splashed with mud, and the boots that had been clean and shiny this morning were filthy. She limped from weariness, and Chase figured that Amelia had never spent such a miserable day. Yet she hadn't complained once, and sympathy for Willie Honaker had brought tears to her eyes.

Chase knew that thinking of "what might have been" was futile, but momentarily he wondered what their lives would be like now if their marriage hadn't failed and they'd continued to live together.

Amelia slipped in the mud, and he reached a hand to help her. She steadied herself without his assistance and moved on, unaware that he was watching her. Chase knew he couldn't redeem the past, but what did he want from Amelia now? Was it too late for them to start over? Did he want another chance with Amelia?

While the idea stirred his emotions, he questioned if Amelia would welcome an opportunity to start over. He recalled her words when they'd left the lawyer's office on the day their divorce had been finalized.

"When we married, Chase, I meant it when I said, "Til death do us part.' But I couldn't see any way out except for a divorce, and I'm glad it's over. Please stay out of my life. I don't want to see you again."

He'd taken Amelia at her word and had made no effort to contact her. Had time caused a change in her feelings toward him, or did she still feel the same way?

Chapter Four

The sun rose brightly the next morning, and the water had receded enough so that two kitchen vans had come across the West Virginia border into the flooded area. One van had set up in the parking lot of Mountainview Church, and the cooks would have hot food ready to deliver by noon.

Other volunteers had arrived, too. When Amelia learned that a route was open northward, she told Rick Smith she wanted to go to Charleston to get her Buick, when space was available in a vehicle to take her there.

Chase heard the conversation, and offered, "I'll be going that way tomorrow. We're taking the church's truck home. I'll stay in Worthington for a few days to get my work organized so others can carry on for a few weeks, and then I'll come back. You can ride into Charleston with us, Amelia."

Wishing heartily that he would leave her alone, she said, "We'll see."

Water had receded from the hollow where Josh and Mandy Newberry lived, and since the old couple wanted to go home, Rick asked Chase and Amelia to take them. It wasn't an assignment Amelia welcomed. For one thing, she didn't want to spend another day with Chase. And if the Newberrys' home had been destroyed like those she'd seen yesterday, what words could she find to comfort Mandy and Josh?

Amelia helped Mandy choose cleaning necessities from the supplies sent from Chase's church and by many local churches. Then she packaged the items Mandy chose and carried them for her. Instead of the Jeep, Chase was assigned to drive a four-seat pickup truck, and he helped Amelia pack the supplies in the truck bed.

The prospects of going home had brought smiles of pleasure to the work-worn faces of Josh and Mandy. They settled into the back seat of the truck, their hands clasped.

When Chase started the truck's engine, Rick Smith peered in the open door and shook hands with Josh and Mandy.

"Staying in a damp building can make you sick, so after you clean the house, come back and stay at the shelter for several days until the house has time to dry." Before he closed their door, Rick turned his attention to Amelia and Chase. "Don't leave them out there."

Chase nodded, but Amelia made no comment. One glance at the satisfied expressions on the Newberrys' faces convinced her that it wasn't likely they'd leave their home again.

After several miles of travel on a paved road that occasionally provided a view of the swollen Tug Fork River, following Josh's instructions, Chase turned the truck into the narrow hollow where the Newberrys lived. At first, the elderly couple silently observed the devastation of the countryside. A lump built in Amelia's throat when Josh started singing in an unsteady tenor voice that must have been strong and melodious in his youth. "God is so good, He's so good to me."

Amelia believed that her faith was strong, but if there was a possibility that her home and all her possessions had been destroyed, could she sing "God Is So Good"? In spite of her disappointing marriage, Amelia knew she'd been extremely fortunate, but how would she react if another tragedy struck her life? She started singing with Josh, trying with all her might to believe in the goodness of God, regardless of the circumstances.

Only ten families lived in the hollow, and Chase and Amelia came first to the property of the Newberrys' neighbors. All of the mobile homes had been washed off their foundations, and many of the frame buildings leaned precariously toward the creek.

"Our home is next, at the head of the holler," Mandy said excitedly.

They rounded the bend, and Josh shouted, "Praise God, the house still stands! Mandy, the house still stands!" He threw his arms around his little wife and hugged her tightly. When Chase stopped before the flooded house, Josh opened the door, jumped sprightly to the muddy ground and reached inside to lift Mandy out.

With Josh's arm firmly around Mandy's waist, they stood and surveyed the house as if it were a mansion. Unable to comprehend their joy, Amelia glanced at Chase with incredulous eyes. Precipitous mountain terrain surrounded the little farm. Even before it flooded, their acreage couldn't have been comfortable, at least by most standards. And now, blooming daffodils and tulips had toppled to the ground, covered with mud. The posts of the yard fence had been washed out by the rushing water and the wire was flattened.

She considered her apartment to be small, but this house would easily fit into her apartment, with room to spare. Amelia assumed that the small shack behind the house, with a half-moon carved in the door, was the plumbing system, unless the lean-to with an air vent, attached to the house, was a bathroom. Several outbuildings, some washed off their foundations, were scattered around the clearing.

"Sad, isn't it?" Chase murmured, his deep sympathy revealed in his eyes. "We might as well see what we can do to help them."

Josh explained that the flood had come at night, and the Newberrys hadn't known the creek was rising until their nearest neighbor pounded on the door.

"It hadn't rained much right here, so I hadn't been worried. But there was a cloudburst up on the mountain. I pulled on a pair of britches, and Mandy put a dress over her nightgown, and we climbed in his truck," Josh said. "The creek was already runnin' in the kitchen door, and it chased us all the way down the holler. God only knows how we made it to the high road before the water caught us."

About five feet of water had rushed through the house, but it wasn't as muddy as Willie's house had been. The Newberrys did have antiquated plumbing inside, but the well house had flooded and the electric pump was probably ruined. All electricity in the area was out of service, so the lights wouldn't work, either.

Mandy wiped tears from her eyes as she picked up two soaked picture albums. The memories of a lifetime had been destroyed in a matter of minutes.

"One of our daughters sent us word while we were in the shelter, and she said she'd replace as many of the pictures as she could. But I ought not to mourn over pictures when all of my family is safe.''

With water carried from a spring on the mountainside, the four of them scrubbed the floor of the house with disinfectant and strong soap. Except for the kitchen table and chairs, the rest of the furniture was ruined. Josh and Chase carried it outside. A wood-burning stove in the living room was cleaned, and, bringing wood from a stack near the barn, Josh started a fire. After scrubbing a metal pan, Mandy heated spring water so they could have a hot drink with their lunch.

''Let's go up on the hill and have a picnic,'' Mandy said, ''and give the house a chance to dry out a little.''

Go on a picnic when all their household possessions had been destroyed! Amelia and Chase exchanged wry smiles as they gathered sandwiches, cookies, drinks and disposable cups from the truck and followed the Newberrys up the mountain to a fairly level spot under a gnarled oak tree. A few boulders littered the area and, following the Newberrys' example, Chase and Amelia sat on the rocks.

Josh removed his battered hat and lowered his head. ''Lord, for Your goodness we thank You. You've been good to us—brought us safely through the flood, just like You did ole Noah. We've got so much to thank You for, God, that I don't know where to start countin'. Right now, thank You for this food and for Chase and Amelia, who're so good to help us. Amen.''

Amelia wiped away tears before she passed sandwiches and fruit to everyone. ''But what are you going to *do?*'' she asked. ''You've lost everything.''

''No, no, my dear!'' Mandy said, patting Amelia's hand. ''We ain't lost everything. The house is still here, and so's the barn. I see my flock of chickens scratchin' around the farm. The cows and sheep are safe. We'll come around all right.''

Josh laid a caressing hand on Mandy's shoulder. ''And we have each other,'' he said tenderly.

''How long have you been married?'' Chase asked.

''More'n sixty-five years. Mandy was only fifteen when I married her. I was two years older.''

Waving his hand to encompass the Newberrys' home, Chase said, ''You couldn't have had an easy life, yet you seem happy. Do you have any regrets?''

''Only a few,'' Josh said. ''I worked on the railroad most of my life and retired with a good pension. I was away a lot of the time, but Mandy took care of our home and raised the kids. I missed a lot of time with my kids when they were growing up. Thanks to their mama, they're good young'uns, too. Soon as they can, they'll be here to help us rebuild. By the time I retired, the kids had all left home, so Mandy and me had time to ourselves. Been just like a second honeymoon.'' He winked at Mandy.

"How could it be a second honeymoon when we didn't even have the first one?" she said pertly.

Their evident affection baffled Amelia. In this isolated hollow, she was witnessing marriage at its best.

Chase must have been as perplexed as Amelia, for he said, "Haven't you ever had a fight?"

Josh's hearty laugh echoed around the hollow. "Oh, sure! Now and ag'in we've fought."

With a sly grin, Mandy said, "But it's always so much fun to make up."

"Either of you been married?" Josh asked.

A soft gasp escaped Amelia's lips, and Chase glanced her way. Her head was bowed, and her face colored in embarrassment.

"Yes," Chase answered easily. "Both of us have been married, but we're divorced."

"Aw, that's too bad," Mandy said. "A good marriage is one of the best blessings God can give." She shook her head sadly. "Too bad."

Perhaps sensing Amelia's discomfort, Josh said, "Let's get back to our work, Mandy. There's a lot to be done before nightfall."

"Surely you're going back to the shelter with us," Chase said.

"No, we'll do fine here," Mandy said.

"You don't have a bed, and the floor is cold and damp," Amelia protested.

Mandy smiled tenderly at Amelia. "Thanks for worrying about us, Amelia, but we'll manage.

We've got some clean, dry bales of hay in the barn. We can cover them with the blankets we brought from town. With the fire, we'll be warm enough. We've been separated for several nights—women in one part of the gym, men in the other. I'd rather stay here—I just don't rest well if Josh ain't by my side.''

"You go on now and help others who need more'n we do," Josh said. "If you'll carry some wood and put it on the front porch, we'll be all right. We've got enough food and water to do for a few days. By then, our kids will be here to help us."

In spite of Josh's urging, Amelia and Chase didn't leave until after they'd piled several days' supply of wood on the porch and had scrubbed the table and chairs, the kitchen sink and cabinets.

"We'll be back in a few days," Chase promised as they got in the truck.

Waving to the Newberrys, who watched their departure from the littered yard, Amelia said, "They look very lonely. I'm sorry to leave them."

Chase laughed, and with an impish gleam in his eyes, he glanced at Amelia. "Frankly, I think they're glad to get rid of us."

"What?"

"I mean it. They're used to being alone. Probably days go by and they see no one else. For almost a week, they've been penned up with lots of people, day and night. They don't need anyone except each other.''

''Probably you're right. I spend a lot of time alone, too, and I feel crowded sleeping in the same room with Vicky.''

They traveled in silence until they'd cleared the hollow and were on the paved highway headed for Williamson.

''The Newberrys prove that marriages can be successful,'' Chase said. ''We should have asked for advice on how to make a marriage work.''

Tension tightened the muscles in Amelia's stomach. She didn't know where Chase was going with that comment, so she didn't answer. Instead, she examined her hands. The nails were broken, and a blister had formed on her right palm when she was scrubbing the kitchen table. While she was carrying wood, she'd gotten a splinter in her left hand. Chase had tenderly removed the splinter and applied ointment to the injury, but an angry-looking wound remained. Amelia hadn't gotten weekly manicures since she'd started supporting herself, but she always gave daily attention to her nails. If her hands looked like this after two days, what condition would they be in at the end of three weeks?

Apparently reading her thoughts, Chase said, ''We should have worn rubber gloves—for safety, if nothing else. Maybe you should see a doctor about that wound—you don't want to get an infection.''

"I'll watch it, and put some antibiotic ointment on when we get back."

When they approached a pizza restaurant, Chase said, "Shall we stop here and eat?"

"I'm so tired, all I want to do is go to bed, but some hot food might refresh me."

Chase parked the truck, but before he turned off the ignition, he said, "Amelia, we can't go on acting like strangers. We were married and lived together for five years—we can't erase those memories."

"I have," she said bitterly, knowing in her heart that she wasn't being completely truthful. "And since you're planning to continue working here, I'm going to tell Rick to separate us. He can think whatever he wants. The emotional turmoil between us is upsetting. I can't give myself wholeheartedly to disaster relief when your presence keeps reminding me of things I thought I'd forgotten."

"I can't believe you have nothing left except bad memories. We had some good times together."

She turned on him and unleashed the hurt that she'd bottled up for years. "Yes, but the humiliation and degradation I endured while you openly had an affair with Rosemary wiped out any happy memories I had. How do you think I felt to have you destroy our wedding vows in front of the whole town?"

"But you didn't even act like you cared. You wouldn't talk about it."

"What did you expect me to do, grovel at your feet, beg you to be a faithful husband? After I learned about your infidelity, I didn't have much pride left, but I still had some. I loved you and thought you loved me—at least, you made a good pretense of it."

"I *did* love you. But when I asked your forgiveness, you turned frigid and wouldn't let me touch you."

She cast a scornful glance at him, her breath came in gulps and her hands shook. "It's obvious we can't continue working together. If two days with you has upset me this much, I can't bear three weeks of it. Let's go. I don't feel like eating."

Amelia was appalled at the viciousness pouring from her mouth. She couldn't stop. The words had accumulated for years and had suddenly burst forth like an artesian well. Even in the final weeks of their marriage, when they'd lived apart under the same roof, they'd never quarreled.

"You made me the laughingstock in town. How you could expect me to welcome you home with open arms when you'd been sleeping with Rosemary is something I could never understand."

"You could at least have listened to an explanation."

She glared at him, her dark brown eyes burning and accusing. Even her long, curly eyelashes seemed to bristle with indignation.

Chase threw up his hands. "Okay, okay. I won't say anything more. Do you want me to go back to Ohio and stay there?"

"Do what you want to. I'm committed to stay for three weeks, but this disaster area is widespread. We can work in different locations. I don't want to work where you do."

Chase's gray eyes darkened like angry thunderclouds, and the glance he tossed at her was like a bolt of lightning. The strained silence between them was unbearable as they continued their journey.

Chapter Five

Amelia stared fixedly out the side window, wondering how she could endure spending any more time in Chase's company.

Lord, I want to continue the work I volunteered to do, but I can't risk seeing Chase every day. What can I do?

Her prayer was answered quickly, because, when they drove into the church's parking lot, Rick ran toward them.

"Amelia, a helicopter is leaving in about fifteen minutes for Charleston, to take a severely injured man to the trauma center there. There's room for you to ride along if you want to go pick up your car. I'll take you up to the hospital where the 'copter is waiting."

"Give me five minutes to get my purse from the

room.'' She didn't even glance toward Chase, but ran into the church and upstairs to the room she shared with Vicky. She was back in less time than she'd asked for.

The helicopter was ready to take off when Rick reached the landing pad.

"Thanks, Rick," she called as she sprinted toward the helicopter. "I'll be back tomorrow."

The pilot lifted into the air as soon as Amelia was settled into the 'copter beside the sick man and the medical team that accompanied him.

She supposed she shouldn't have left Chase without a word, but they'd already said too much in the past hour. After suppressing her anger against him for so many years, why had she suddenly vented her hurt feelings? Did she still love Chase in spite of what he'd done to her? If she was indifferent to her ex-husband, why had she become so angry?

Amelia folded her knees, wrapped her arms around them and leaned her head on her knees.

God, I'm so confused. I was convinced it was Your will for me to volunteer for this mission. After only two days, I'm ready to pack up and go home. I think I could have handled the stress and devastation of the disaster if I hadn't encountered Chase. Why did You bring us together again?

Her mind flashed back to their wedding day, and the minister's words, ''Therefore what God has joined together, let man not separate.'' In the eyes of God, were Chase and she still man and wife?

Since she'd become a Christian and believed that marriage was God-ordained, it had bothered her often that her marriage had failed. But the Bible taught that divorce was acceptable when a spouse was unfaithful. Besides, what else could she have done? As the helicopter whirred its way northward, Amelia recalled the events that had wrecked her marriage.

Rosemary Taylor had been one of the girls who'd competed with Amelia for Chase's affections. He'd dated Rosemary several times before he'd met Amelia. When Chase started dating Amelia exclusively, Rosemary wouldn't take their relationship seriously. Right up until the day they were married, Rosemary kept trying to win Chase away from Amelia. Soon after their marriage, Chase and Amelia had moved to another town in central Kansas, and Amelia thought her problems with Rosemary were over.

Four years later, however, Rosemary turned up in their town and took a job in the company where Chase worked. Amelia was a little apprehensive, but Chase didn't show any interest in his former girlfriend. Then one Saturday, Chase had gone to a business meeting with Rosemary in another town. Amelia had expected him to come home that night, but he hadn't. He wasn't acting like himself when he returned the next day, though he explained that they'd had car trouble that delayed them. He said he'd tried to telephone and couldn't get in touch with her.

A few days later, Amelia heard that Chase and Rosemary had spent the night together. He didn't deny it when she confronted him about it, saying it was true, but he was sorry it had happened.

Amelia and Chase continued to live in the same house, but after a month she couldn't bear it any longer and sued for divorce. Chase hadn't objected. Amelia moved back to her parents' home in another city, leaving their lawyers to hammer out the details. Neither of them had been vindictive about the settlement, and since there was no contest to the divorce, no children to be considered, and they agreed on equal distribution of their assets, four months after she'd learned of Chase's unfaithfulness, the divorce had been finalized.

Amelia had drawn a curtain over the past. She'd left her parents' home at their suggestion, moved to another location to find a job and had started a new life. The past few days, the curtain had gapped a little, and she'd peered into the past again. But after the harsh words they'd exchanged this afternoon, she figured the curtain had not only closed, but that a padlock had been put on it.

As the helicopter hovered over the landing field in Charleston, Amelia acknowledged that her relationship with Chase was over at last. Since that was what she wanted, why was she overwhelmed by deep despair and inner torment?

Chase watched Amelia race from the church without sparing one backward glance for him, as if a pack of bloodhounds nipped at her heels. He'd given Amelia up once, believing it was forever, but in the past two days, he'd started thinking it was possible for them to patch up their differences.

He walked to the edge of the church's parking lot and looked toward the hollow where the hospital was located. He waited until he saw the helicopter lift from the ground and head north. Chase sighed, knowing that a lonely future awaited him. He'd created a life without Amelia, and if he hadn't encountered her again, he believed he would have been content even if he wasn't happy. After a few hours of Amelia's company, his contentment was gone. How could he win her love again?

He wearily climbed the stairs to the room he shared with his friend Newt, who'd come with him to the disaster area. Newt lounged on a cot, listening to a tape through earphones.

"As far as I'm concerned," Chase said, "we can go home tonight."

"I'm pretty tired, Chase. I've been pushing mud off the streets of Welsh all day."

"I'll do the driving. You can sleep while we

travel. If we start soon, we can be home by midnight."

"Then let's get started," Newt agreed. "I'm homesick for my wife and kids."

Newt's words served to emphasize Chase's loneliness. He seldom found any pleasure in going home. During the week, when he was home only long enough to sleep and have breakfast, the silence in the house was bearable. On weekends, he volunteered for any church or civic activity he could find—anything to get away from his empty house.

Chase and Newt were soon on their way northward, and it was a relief to Chase when his friend went to sleep. He wasn't in the mood to talk; in fact, he wasn't in a mood to do anything. During their years together, Amelia had never talked to him the way she had today. Did she hate him that much? He would have thought that, after all these years, her anger would have cooled. Did he deserve her hatred? He probably did. Apparently Amelia had never forgiven him, which wasn't surprising, because he wasn't even sure he'd forgiven himself.

Chase had enjoyed being married and having a home. Since the divorce, he'd considered finding another potential bride several times, but he always stopped short of asking anyone to marry him. Was that because no one compared to Amelia? Or because he couldn't trust himself to be faithful to another wife?

From his point of view, they'd had a successful marriage, and he had believed that Amelia felt the same way. Their emotional life was more than satisfactory, and he'd never been tempted to see another woman after he'd started dating her. So why had he gotten involved with Rosemary?

After Rosemary had started working where he did, she'd thrown out several offers, but he hadn't been tempted. Since they were business associates, he couldn't ignore her completely. Even though Amelia was going through an emotional crisis and had been living in a world of her own that didn't include him, he hadn't been apprehensive when he'd accompanied Rosemary to an out-of-town conference, because he had no interest in a relationship with her.

As the miles passed in tune to the powerful surge of the eighteen-wheeler, he speculated about the trip with Rosemary that had doomed his marriage.

Rosemary had driven, and on the return trip, her car had developed a problem, which had caused an overnight delay. They'd had dinner together before he telephoned Amelia, but she didn't answer the phone, even though he'd told her he would call. He was lonely and hurt, and when Rosemary had suggested that they rent only one room, he hadn't objected.

The next morning, he was contrite and told Rosemary that he'd been wrong and apologetically said, "Don't expect this to happen again. I love Amelia."

Chase hadn't decided if he should confess his mistake to Amelia until the news circulated that he and Rosemary had been seen together leaving the motel. Amelia was hurt and full of disbelief when she heard the story, and when he admitted what had happened and asked her forgiveness, she absolutely refused to listen to his explanation. But even if Rosemary had staged their initial encounter, he had no one to blame—except himself—for continuing to see her. At the time, he'd used Amelia's coldness to justify his actions, but he should have been man enough to refuse Rosemary's frequent advances.

He'd had no intention of marrying Rosemary, although she'd assumed that was inevitable when Amelia sued for divorce. He'd stopped seeing Rosemary before his divorce was finalized, because after Amelia and he had separated, he had asked for a transfer to another branch of his company, located in Chicago. He hadn't seen Rosemary since he'd left Kansas. After a few years in Chicago, he moved to Ohio.

The past was gone, and he couldn't dwell on it, but what should he do now? Was his desire to return to West Virginia generated by his compassion for those who'd lost so much, or was he more influenced by an excuse to prolong his reunion with Amelia? If that was the case, since she obviously didn't want a reconciliation, he might as well forget the flood victims and return to work. On the other hand, if God was calling him to help with the cleanup in the disaster area, shouldn't he go despite Amelia's ultimatum?

After she reclaimed her car at Yeager Airport, Amelia drove into Charleston and registered at a motel. She hadn't had a shower or a real bath for days, and the first thing she did was throw aside her dirty clothes, run a tub full of hot water and soak for forty-five minutes. Thinking of the poor living conditions of the residents, as well as the volunteers, in the flooded area, Amelia felt downright guilty luxuriating in such comfort. But she knew that staying dirty wouldn't help any of the others, so she enjoyed the bath and changed into clean garments. Then she went to the motel's coin laundry and washed her dirty clothes. After asking directions from the motel clerk, she drove to the Town Center Mall to have dinner, where she also bought additional underwear for herself and several things for Vicky, too.

After she returned to the motel, she telephoned her parents' condo at Hilton Head. She hadn't tried to call them before she left Philadelphia, thinking she could do it when she arrived at her destination, not realizing how limited outside communications would be in the flooded area.

Usually she had to leave a message when she telephoned home because her parents were usually not home to answer the phone. They were involved in a variety of civic activities. They also had a host of friends with whom they traveled and shared dinner.

To Amelia's surprise, her mother answered the phone.

"Hello, Mother," Amelia said. "How are you and Dad?"

"Fine. I'm glad you called, because I intended to contact you this week. We're going on a ten-day Caribbean cruise in two weeks to celebrate your father's seventy-fifth birthday. Several of our friends are going with us."

This information stung a little—shouldn't an only child have been invited to observe this milestone of her father? But she merely answered, without rancor, "Have a good time."

"I'm sure we will. We like cruises. Everything all right with you?"

Amelia laughed lightly, knowing the revelation of her present whereabouts would come like a bomb blast to her mother.

"Yes, and no," she said. "I'm in West Virginia now!"

"What? Not where that flood is, I hope."

Apparently news of the flood was widespread.

"That's right. I've been here several days already. I came as a Red Cross volunteer."

"Amelia! What have you been doing? Where are you now?"

She briefly explained her activities over the past few days—her drive from Philadelphia and the flight into the flooded area.

"I came to Charleston in a helicopter today to pick up my car. I'll return to the disaster area tomorrow morning."

"I knew when you started working for the Red Cross, you'd be involved in that sort of thing."

"I remember you predicted that, but I've been working for the Red Cross for several years, and up until now, I've only had a soft office job. I decided it was time to be involved more directly in field-work, and here I am."

"For how long?"

"I volunteered for three weeks, but depending on circumstances, it may be longer."

"I've never understood how Alex and I produced a child like you."

Amelia could sense her mother shaking her head in dismay. At one time, this attitude would have devastated Amelia, but, for her own peace of mind, she'd finally accepted her parents as they were. She knew she couldn't change them any more than they could change her.

"I've often wondered that myself, Mother."

"Oh, well, be careful."

Amelia told her mother where she could be reached in case of an emergency, adding, "For the time being, however, phone service is limited, but if necessary, you can contact the state police. They could get a message to me.''

She could imagine only a few reasons why her parents would contact her, but she wouldn't want them worried if they did need her

Amelia's phone calls to her parents didn't usually last long since they had so little in common, but tonight she seemed reluctant to end the conversation. After being with Chase for a few days, was she lonely without him? Why couldn't she stop thinking about him?

"You'll never guess whom I met in the flood area," Amelia said.

"If I can't guess, then you'll have to tell me."

"Chase."

A momentarily silence followed her mother's soft gasp.

"Chase? Chase Ramsey?"

"Yes. He's living in Ohio now, and he brought supplies from his church for the flood victims. We met the first day I arrived here."

Excitedly, Mrs. Stone asked, "Well, how is the dear boy? I think of him often. What's he doing?"

Thinking that her mother was more interested in Chase than her own daughter, Amelia explained briefly about Chase's job and where he was working.

"Has he remarried?"

"No."

"Then I hope you'll not let him get away from you again, Amelia. Surely you've realized, during these past years, what a good husband Chase was."

Amelia had never criticized Chase to her parents, and had allowed them to come to their own conclusions as to what caused the divorce.

"Did you hear me, Amelia?"

"Sure, Mother, I heard you, but I don't know how to answer you. I'm getting along all right as I am—I doubt there's any need for a change. Please don't expect a reconciliation between us."

"Well, it's your life, but I warn you, it won't be pleasant growing old alone. Is there anything else? We have guests coming."

"No, I guess not. I only wanted you to know where I am."

"I appreciate that. Let us know when you return to Philadelphia. If we aren't home from the cruise, you can leave word on our answering machine. Bye."

As always, Amelia had a let-down feeling when she finished talking to her mother.

She started south toward the disaster area early the next morning, wondering if she'd meet Chase on his way to Ohio. She experienced a deep disappointment when she didn't meet his truck. She'd made it plain that she didn't want anything to do with him, so she doubted that he would return to work with the cleanup activities. Would it be another fifteen years before she saw Chase again? She shuddered at the thought. They'd both be fifty-eight by then, because not only had they shared a marriage, they shared a birthday date.

Many roads were still impassable, blocked by rock slides, destroyed bridges and pavement, so she had to make several detours to reach the Williamson area. She didn't arrive at Mountainview Church until late in the afternoon.

When she entered the basement, Vicky called to her from the office area. "I'm glad you're back. The Red Cross has reserved a four-story motel in Williamson for their volunteers. I told them we could room together, and we can move in anytime. I already have two keys to a room on the second floor. Since you've gotten your car, it will be easier to have a room of our own and still have transportation back and forth to Red Cross headquarters." She peeked up at Amelia, her heavily lashed blue eyes sparkling mischievously. "I assume you'll let me ride in your car and share a room with you."

"Well, I'll think about it, but it depends on your behavior."

"Oh, I'll behave. I'll promise anything to have a room with a comfortable bed and a bathroom. I suppose I am soft, as my dad told me, but I'm longing for a long soak in a hot tub of water."

"Which I had last night, and it was wonderful. Now my conscience won't hurt so much when I know you and the other volunteers will soon have the same luxury. Just think—only a few days ago, we took daily baths for granted!''

As they gathered their possessions from the upstairs classroom and carried them to the car, Vicky said, ''I sent Mom a note by Mr. Ramsey, asking her to send some more clothes to me if anyone else from the church comes to help. The clothing I brought with me isn't very practical if I do any work outside the office.''

Amelia handed Vicky the bag of clothes she'd bought in Charleston. ''I went shopping last night and picked up a few things for you. I hope I guessed your size right.''

Vicky looked at her in amazement. ''What a nice thing to do.''

She excitedly pulled the clothes from the bag. Sadly Amelia wondered how long it had been since she'd been that excited about anything.

Amelia had bought two pairs of pull-on cotton pants, one a faded blue, the other khaki. And to complete the outfit, she'd chosen a blue heather cotton-and-polyester mock turtleneck top and a dark blue plaid flannel shirt. She'd also added several pair of cotton underpants.

''You're wonderful!'' Vicky said, flinging her arms around Amelia and giving her a bear hug. ''Thanks. Let's hurry to the motel, so I can try them on.''

''What time did Chase and his friend leave this

morning?'' Amelia said, trying to seem nonchalant as they left the church and walked to her car.

''Oh, they left last night. Mr. Ramsey didn't know if he'd return, but if he does, he's promised to bring more clothes for me. He's a nice guy. He and Dad are good friends, and Mom invites him for dinner often.''

''How long have you known him?''

''He joined our church as soon as he moved to Worthington. I don't remember how long he's been there. He's a dynamo of activity—he coaches the men's softball team, and he's gone on several mission tours to Latin American countries. He'll do anything that has to be done. Dad says it's a good thing he isn't married, or Chase wouldn't have time for all of those extra activities.''

Vicky's comments gave Amelia new things to contemplate. Both Chase and she seemed to be making a contribution to society in their own way. But remembering her husband's former attitude about spiritual matters, she wondered if he really had changed as much as it seemed. Amelia was sorry to remember the saying, ''A leopard can't change its spots.'' She wanted to believe the best about Chase, but should she even entertain thoughts of them being together again?

Chapter Six

The Sycamore Inn was luxury compared to the crowded room they'd been sharing with other volunteers. There were two double beds, two bedside tables, a desk and two straight chairs, as well as one padded lounge chair that faced the television.

"We'll have to take turns in the easy chair," Vicky said.

"Oh, I won't fight you for it," Amelia said. "Most of the time when I watch TV, I lie on the bed with pillows propped behind my back. Often, I go to sleep and forget to turn the television off, and it's on all night."

After Vicky enjoyed a hot bath and changed into the new clothes Amelia had bought for her, they walked next door to the Brass Tree Restaurant for their evening meal. Vicky seemed unusually quiet when they returned to the motel, and it wasn't long before she said, "I'm going to bed. It's going to be wonderful to stretch out on a comfortable mattress. Dad may be right—maybe I wouldn't make a good missionary."

"Being a missionary wouldn't necessarily take you into the jungle. You can be a missionary and never leave the United States. If God calls you to a particular task, He'll also provide the way."

Amelia was tired, too, and she went to bed and turned out the light. Her joints and muscles hadn't yet adjusted to the strenuous work she'd been doing, and she hoped for a restful night's sleep. But stress over the needs of the local residents, as well as her tumultuous reunion with Chase, was taking a toll. She couldn't relax enough to become sleepy.

Amelia soon became aware that Vicky kept turning and twisting in bed. Then she heard the undeniable sound of sniffing.

Amelia leaned on one elbow and looked toward her companion. "Are you all right, Vicky?"

"I don't know," Vicky said tearfully. "I suppose I'm homesick. I wish my mother was here."

"Anything I can do?"

"Maybe. I just need a heart-to-heart chat with Mom. Maybe you can take her place."

Amelia figured that was unlikely, but she said, "I've never had any experience being a mom, but I can listen, even if I don't have advice to give."

"Do you believe in love at first sight?"

Amelia sat up suddenly. Had something been going on in front of her eyes, and she'd been too involved in her own problems to notice? Of course, she hadn't spent much time around headquarters at Mountainview Church where Vicky worked all day.

"I've heard many people say that they've fallen in love at first sight," Amelia answered slowly. "Although it hasn't happened to me, I can't dispute the word of people who say they've experienced an immediate attraction to someone."

"Then you have been in love?" Vicky persisted.

Amelia didn't like the direction this conversation was heading.

"Well…yes."

"But it wasn't instantaneous?"

Amelia thought of the first time she'd met Chase. She'd been attracted to him, but it was several months after their first date when she'd realized that she did love him.

"Amelia?"

"I was thinking. I remember several cases of love when I was a child. I had crushes on one of my schoolteachers and my doctor."

"Oh, I had those, too," Vicky said impatiently. "I mean an adult love when you meet an eligible man—someone your own age—and you immediately know he's the right person for you."

"Not the first time I met the person. It didn't come like a bolt out of the blue."

"How did you know? How did you feel?"

Because she'd tried for years to suppress her feelings for Chase, it wasn't easy to recall her emotions of twenty years ago.

As she reminisced, Amelia forgot that Vicky was in the room. "It seemed as if my life had been a long treasure hunt, as if I was looking for something precious. I'd looked everywhere for what I needed to make my life complete, and when I met—" She hesitated. "When I realized I was in love with this man, it was as if my search was over at last. He filled a space in my heart that had always been empty."

Amelia realized that Vicky was very silent, as if she listened intently. Fleetingly, she hoped that Vicky wasn't putting two and two together and coming up with the identity of the man Amelia had loved. But immersed as she was in the past, she continued, "Since then, I've read a Native American legend indicating that each soul is born incomplete, and that people wander over the earth looking for their other half. It's only when you find the other half of yourself that you can be happy. I know that isn't biblical, but I think it's a beautiful thought."

"It is beautiful, but kinda sad, too, especially if you live all of your life without finding your 'other' half. Though I suppose it's worth waiting if you do find the perfect mate.''

''That's what the wedding service means when it says 'two will become one flesh.' Anyone is fortunate if they find their 'other half.'''

Suddenly, Amelia felt tears seeping from her closed eyelids, and she lay flat on her back while bitter remorse flooded her mind and spirit. She'd once had her ''other half,'' and she'd turned her back on him, not once but twice. She'd heard of having a *second* chance, but not a *third* one.

''I'm sorry,'' Vicky said. ''I didn't mean to make you sad.''

''I'm sorry, too, that I didn't make a very good mom to you. But I'm all right now—go ahead with your problem. Do you want to tell me who you're attracted to?''

''Allen Chambers.''

''Oh, the pastor! He's a very nice man, but a bit old for you, isn't he?''

''I think he's about thirty. But age shouldn't matter, should it? The man you loved—what difference was there in ages?''

''None at all. We shared the same birthday. But I'd rather not talk about my situation. That's a part of the past. Let's deal with your problem. Does Allen share your feelings?''

''I don't know. He hasn't given me any reason to believe he cares for me.''

"Then take it slow, Vicky. If you say anything, and he isn't interested, you'll be very embarrassed. That's about the only advice I can give you."

"I believe that God has called me into full-time Christian service of some kind. I thought that meant I'd be a missionary. But being a preacher's wife ought to fit in that category, don't you think?"

"I'm sure it would, but pray about your decision. You're testing the waters of volunteer service now, so that may be the kind of work He wants you to do. When we move ahead and try to outguess God, we get into trouble."

As she spoke, Amelia wondered if this wasn't good advice, which she also should follow.

"Thanks, Amelia. You've made me feel a lot better. I can go to sleep now, I think."

Soon, Vicky was breathing easily, and Amelia knew she'd gone to sleep, but it was a long time before Amelia stopped agonizing over her own perplexing emotions. Disquieting thoughts raced through her mind. Regardless of who'd caused the breach between Chase and her, if she wanted to reclaim her marriage, should she take the initiative? Chase had hinted that he wanted to be with her again. Was it time to put away her hurt pride and reconcile?

Believing that he did want to help the unfortunate, as well as see more of Amelia, two days later, Chase arranged to take his vacation days and returned to southern West Virginia. The floodwaters had receded and the cleanup was in full force, although several small communities were still isolated because the bridges and roads to their towns had been destroyed. Hundreds of volunteers from all over the country had converged on the area.

Most of the volunteers had been housed in motels by now, although the gymnasium at Mountainview Church was still being used by the Red Cross as headquarters for staff workers and supply storage. The mobile kitchen was operating from the church's parking lot, because many people still needed daily food deliveries. Under the direction of two female dietitians, men cooked food under large tents. Smaller tents were set up where volunteers could have their meals, and Chase joined several of them for a cup of coffee.

Rick Smith walked by and clapped him on the shoulder. "Man, but I'm glad to see you. We need another driver for one of our ERVs. Amelia took it out by herself yesterday, but she wasn't comfortable driving it. And I don't blame her—these rigs are big for narrow roadways."

Chase's pulse quickened when he heard Amelia's name. If she'd transferred to another area as she'd threatened, he'd wondered if he would even see her. "You'd better tell me what an ERV is before I agree to drive it."

Rick motioned to several vehicles, similar to ambulances, parked nearby.

"Those are Emergency Response Vehicles, but we shorten the name to ERV. Some of them are fixed up for ambulance service, and others are used to haul food and supplies. The one I want you to drive is designed to distribute food. You and Amelia will be assigned a regular route to deliver food twice a day."

Chase started to say that he and Amelia wouldn't be working together, but since that was her ultimatum, he'd let her tell Rick that she wouldn't work with him.

"I'm at your service—whatever you want me to do. I brought Vicky several packages from her parents, and I'll be ready as soon as I deliver them. Where can I find her?"

"She's assigned to office work here in the church, but she's staying with Amelia in a motel. They should be here soon."

In a few minutes, Amelia and Vicky drove into the parking lot in a black Park Avenue Ultra. Chase surmised the Buick was Amelia's Christmas gift from her parents, and he whistled. That vehicle had set Mr. Stone back a few dollars! Chase walked in their direction and Vicky opened the passenger door and stepped out.

"Hi," she said. "Did you bring anything from Mom?"

"A whole box full of things. Do you want to put them in the car now? I might not be here when you leave tonight."

Vicky looked at Amelia. "Is it all right to store the box in your car?"

Amelia pushed a button and opened the trunk. "Sure. There's plenty of room back here."

As she walked beside him toward his truck, Vicky said, "I hope Mom sent some more clothes. I'm tired of the few things I brought."

"Yes, she sent clothes, and I heard her mention chocolate-chip cookies."

Vicky squealed. "Oh, great! I'll share with you."

While they were transferring the packages from his truck to her shiny black Buick, Amelia walked away without looking in his direction. Her attitude reminded Chase of the last months of their marriage when Amelia talked to him only when it was necessary. If her unforgiving attitude continued, this tour of duty would seem mighty long. Had he made a mistake in returning to the disaster area?

His thoughts rioted while he answered Vicky's questions about her parents. He tried to keep his mind on what she wanted to know, for he knew it was Vicky's first extended absence from her home. She was probably homesick.

After he'd carried the bags to Amelia's car, Chase said goodbye to Vicky and went to the tent where Rick was making assignments.

"Chase, you and Amelia take the first ERV in line. We've already loaded the insulated containers that are full of hot food. The menu today is meat loaf, mashed potatoes and corn." He pointed to boxes of fruit under one of the tents. "Take a box each of apples and oranges and several boxes of cookies."

Amelia picked up a stack of clamshell disposable containers and carried them toward the ERV Rick had indicated. She still hadn't looked in Chase's direction, but she apparently intended to team with him. When she returned to get a container of iced tea, he lifted the coffee urn and followed her.

The inside of the ERV was well planned. Standing room must have been six feet, for Chase stood up straight with a clearance of an inch or two above his head. The insulated containers, each holding forty quarts of food, were strapped securely on a low table. A plastic bag, containing several blankets and first-aid equipment, was stored between the front seats.

"I'll bring the fruit," Chase said, and without answering him, Amelia made room for the boxes in the ERV and then climbed into the vehicle. There were two commodious bucket seats, one for the pilot and copilot, as the drivers were called.

After Chase got in the van, Rick stood at Amelia's side and gave her a hand-drawn map. "This is basically the same route you took yesterday, Amelia, but you might want the map again today.''

Amelia handed the sketchy map to Chase. He studied it briefly. ''This doesn't look too difficult. I see we're going into the area where the Newberrys live,'' he said.

''I saw them yesterday. They asked about you.''

Chase breathed a silent prayer that she'd finally spoken to him. Her attitude intimidated him, and he'd had no idea how to break down the wall between them.

Rick closed Amelia's door. ''If you finish in time,'' he said, ''you can take another route today, but be careful.''

''We'll be all right,'' Chase replied as he started the engine. He checked out the different driving functions of the vehicle before he drove out of the parking lot. When he accessed the paved highway going east from Williamson, he asked, ''How are the Newberrys?''

A half smile curved Amelia's generous lips. ''Happy as newlyweds,'' she said. ''Some of their children have been to the house and brought enough furniture for a couple of rooms. They're fairly comfortable.''

He passed the map back to her. ''Driving this vehicle is all I can handle. You take the map and give directions. These hollows all look alike to me.''

''After that time I gave you the wrong directions

and you drove seventy-five miles out of our way on the Interstate, you said you'd never let me be the navigator again."

Chase's heartbeat quickened. Amelia had actually made a reference to their past together. And she seemed friendly. What had happened to change her attitude?

But he wasn't going to quibble over the "why," and breathing a silent prayer to God for the change in her, he playfully snatched the paper out of her hand. "You're right—I'd forgotten that. If you send me that far in the wrong direction today, we'll end up in Kentucky or Virginia. Where were we going that day?"

Suddenly, Amelia wished she hadn't made the personal comment. She might have to work with Chase, but she didn't intend to be chummy with him. But considering the overwhelming joy she'd experienced when she'd seen him this morning, it wouldn't be easy to be standoffish with a man who'd once been her devoted husband. The past few days, when it seemed that he'd gone out of her life again, she'd remembered only the good times they'd had together, rather than the humiliating last few months of their marriage.

"We were on our way to Myrtle Beach. Somewhere in Tennessee I told you to take the opposite direction."

Chase tossed the map back toward her. "Oh, I've

forgiven you for that. So help me out today. At least, we can travel this paved road for a while, rather than up over the mountain. Are we going to Willie's place?''

''We're supposed to, but I chickened out yesterday. That road seemed narrow when we were driving a Jeep. I was too scared to take the ERV. I'm sure the road hasn't been repaired so we can't drive to his place yet. We'll have to carry his food to him.''

''Then we should go to Willie first, since that might take a lot of time. I don't see how we can cover all this territory and get back to town in time to start out with a second load.''

''Probably not, but at least we can provide one meal for everyone on our route. Rick knows there's a limit to what we can do.''

After they turned into Willie's hollow, with some difficulty, Chase maneuvered the ERV along the winding, narrow road. When they came to the place where the road was impassable, he turned the vehicle around and parked it where they'd stopped last week.

''Let's fill three of these containers. Willie is obviously a big eater,'' Amelia said.

Chase looked at the sky, wondering if more rain was expected. ''I didn't think to bring a raincoat.''

Amelia reached for her jacket, and Chase took it from her hands and held it for her. She was aware of the tenderness of his touch through the fabric of her jacket. Flustered at his attentions, she said breathlessly, "I don't think you'll need a raincoat. The forecast is for partly cloudy weather today, but more rain is predicted later on in the week."

Chase put the hot food containers and several apples into a plastic box with a handle. Amelia carried a gallon jug of water. Only a few feet of water flowed in the creek bed, and she wasn't as nervous about walking across the narrow stretch of pavement as she had been last week. Chase crossed first, and she was aware of his outstretched, waiting hand, but she ignored it.

Amelia could hardly believe, from this quiet stretch of road with the birds singing and abundant wildflowers blooming on the mountainside, that there was so much devastation in the county. Although they walked side by side, in silence, it was a pleasant walk, and Amelia wasn't aware of any tension between them. For a moment, the intervening years had disappeared and they were man and wife again.

Chapter Seven

They heard Willie's banjo as they crossed the rickety bridge into the little town.

With a happy laugh, Chase said, "It sounds like he's alive and well."

Willie sat on the porch in his rocking chair as he had on their previous visit. His dark eyes gleamed, and his lips parted in a wide smile when he saw them coming. A few of the other houses showed signs of occupancy today.

"Welcome," he said. "I've been lookin' for you. Is the Tug still in flood?"

Chase nodded his head positively. "The river is full from bank to bank, and there's a lot of backwater in the creeks. But it's out of Welsh now."

"Betcha there's a lot of mud."

"A foot or more deep in some places. One of the

coal companies has sent in equipment, and they're using end loaders to put the mud in dump trucks to haul it to the river. That town is a mess—I don't know how they'll ever get ready to open businesses again.''

"They'll have to build a floodwall for protection, like some of the other towns," Willie said.

Conversation was suspended when Willie started eating the warm food.

"Boy, these vittles taste good,'' he said with a wide grin. "My girl, who lives in Kentucky, brought some food a few days back, but I ain't cooked anything.''

"I see that a few of your neighbors have returned to their homes. Are their houses fit to live in?'' Amelia asked.

Willie shook his head. "Some of them ain't. I've heard that the government is gonna provide some trailer houses for the ones that need shelter.''

"That might take a long time,'' Amelia insisted.

"Then we'll just make do until we can fix up the town ourselves.''

As Willie started on his third tray of food, which Amelia had intended for his evening meal, he continued. "It'll surprise you how fast our people bounce back from disasters. In narrow mountain valleys like ours, we expect to be flooded out every once in a while.''

"Then there isn't much incentive for folks to improve their homes,'' Chase said. ''Couldn't they move elsewhere?''

Willie shrugged his shoulders, finished his food, wiped his mouth with the back of his hand and took a big drink of water. ''There's always some who never rebuild after a flood. But this is home, and most of us just stay and take what comes.'' He voiced his thanks for the food they'd brought, then he said, ''Any other problems beside the muddy streets?''

''Mud slides are making a lot of trouble. They block the highways and have caused houses to slide down the mountainsides,'' Amelia said as she handed Willie several apples. ''We've been warned to watch out for them.''

''Yeah,'' Willie agreed. ''The mountains have had all the rain they can stand, 'specially the areas that have been timbered, and there's nothin' left to hold the mud and rocks. You be careful when you're drivin' around.''

While Amelia sat on the edge of the porch and visited with Willie, Chase went to the houses of the others who'd returned and asked them to walk down to the ERV to get their food. When he returned to Amelia, fifteen people came with him and Amelia down the hollow. Instead of taking the food to their homes, the residents opted to eat their meal at the site. They hunkered on the ground or sat on rocks and fallen logs.

"We might as well eat here, too," Chase said. He folded a blanket into a cushion for Amelia to sit on the back ledge of the ERV. He leaned against the vehicle while they ate the surprisingly tasty and nourishing food.

Chase talked easily with the local residents. While Amelia sat quietly, she considered the mission of hundreds of people who'd volunteered to come to southern West Virginia. They were providing physical necessities for the disaster victims, but what about their spiritual needs? These folks had probably lost their Bibles in the high water, and she decided to talk to Rick to see if it would be appropriate to ask her local church to send Bibles to replace the ones they'd lost. But that would take a few weeks. Perhaps they needed spiritual encouragement now.

Amelia disposed of her plate and went to the front of the ERV and took a Bible from her tote bag. She stood beside Chase and cleared her throat nervously, for she was unaccustomed to sharing her faith openly. Chase looked at her, and she said timorously, "If we have time, I might read from the Bible before we leave."

Chase's gold-flecked eyes brightened with pride and another indefinable emotion. "We'll take the time," he said.

Amelia asked the people if they would like for

her to read from the Bible, and their eager acceptance not only testified to their faith, but also their need to hear God's word. What could she read to bring encouragement to her small audience? Asking God to guide her, she turned through the Bible, looking at passages she'd underlined during her private devotions. She paused in the book of Isaiah and read a favorite passage from the forty-first chapter.

"'So do not fear, for I am with you; do not be dismayed, for I am your God. I will strengthen you and help you; I will uphold you and help you; I will uphold you with my righteous right hand.'"

The people before her seemed hungry—not for physical food, for the Red Cross had provided that. They were also hungry for the word of God.

"These words were written to God's people when they were going through a difficult time," Amelia explained. "But I believe the message can be applied to your situation. The present must look very bleak to you, and you probably can't see any hope for the future. I've never experienced the material loss you've had, but I've had emotional difficulties that almost overwhelmed me. With God's help, I overcame those problems, which makes me confident that God will sustain and guide you, if you'll take your troubles to Him."

Amelia was breathless at the end of that short speech, and she looked appealingly at Chase. "Could you give a prayer?"

"Sure," he said, taking her hand, and reaching his other hand to the man nearest to him. "Let's form a prayer circle."

Amelia extended her hand to the child on her right, as the others stood and joined hands with those beside them. Chase's prayer was brief, but he prayed with heartfelt warmth and kindness, asking God to ease the burden of those who'd lost their physical goods. After his amen, Amelia felt compelled to hug the little girl, whose hand she held, and she hugged the other children and women. Chase shook hands with the men, and when they turned to leave, Amelia marveled at the change in the facial expressions of those they'd come to help. Despair had been replaced by hope, and kindness had diminished the bitterness they'd formerly reflected.

"When we minister in the name of the Lord, it makes a difference," Chase said to Amelia as he started the ERV and waved goodbye.

"I couldn't believe the change a few words of encouragement made. I'm glad God prompted me to read the Bible to them."

"I'm proud of you, Amelia."

His gray eyes glowed with warmth, and she blushed at his praise.

"I'm not confident in my ability to speak before groups. I haven't done it before."

"You don't need a lot of experience when you speak from the heart." Sensing a difference in their relationship, Chase found the courage to ask, "Since you've been a Christian, have you ever wondered if our marriage might have turned out differently if we'd brought any spiritual values into it?"

She turned her head sharply to look out the window, and Chase wondered if he'd said the wrong thing. Without looking in his direction, Amelia answered, "The thought has crossed my mind. It's hard to be angry with a person when you hold hands and pray together."

Since he'd made a few inroads into the barrier between them, Chase dared to ask, "Why did you work with me again today when you'd said you wouldn't?"

After a significant pause, she said, "Several reasons. First, I decided I was being childish to let things that happened years ago interfere with the work we're here to do. Also, I don't enjoy conflict with anyone—I never have." She looked shyly toward him, her face flushed, and her voice held a tinge of wonder. "Besides, it's been satisfying to be with you again, Chase. I've missed you the past few days."

Chase's heart glowed with a warmth that melted a cold spot he'd harbored for years. "What about the past fifteen years? Did you miss me then?"

"I forced myself not to miss you. It saddened me to think about you, so I put you out of my mind as much as possible."

"Thanks for forgiving me enough to be my partner. This work can be very depressing, but it helps when we share it. We make a good team—even Rick remarked about that."

"I wonder what he thinks about us."

"He must suspect that we were more than acquaintances, or he wouldn't keep throwing us together. But I'm glad he does—I'd rather work with you than anyone else I know."

Amelia didn't answer. She'd said enough already. She didn't want Chase to get any ideas, because she believed it was impossible for them to turn back the clock to their earlier relationship.

Newberry Hollow was still accessible by vehicles, since the hillsides were heavily timbered and no landslides had closed the road. At each home they passed, wrecked buildings were being restored to their foundations. Piles of damaged household items stood in front of each building, and families were inside cleaning the walls and floors. Noting the extent of the damage, Amelia wondered where they would find enough furniture for their basic needs. But since she couldn't provide everything, with a cheerful smile and a friendly attitude, she dispensed the food they'd brought.

It was midafternoon when they drove into the Newberrys' yard, and Amelia said, "We'll never get back in time to make another run. I hope Rick understands.''

''I'm sure he will. He's been the Red Cross director in this area for several years. He knows it isn't always possible to keep on a schedule. If all we did was serve food, we could make time, but these people need to talk as much as they need to eat. And I couldn't turn down that little lady who asked us to help move her furniture.''

Amelia was impressed more and more by Chase's compassion. During their years of marriage, they'd been so wrapped up in each other that they hadn't reached out to anyone else. Being together had fulfilled their needs. But now she was seeing another side to Chase—a genuine concern for those who'd lost so much.

They were delayed even more at the Newberrys, because the elderly couple insisted that Amelia and Chase should ''sit a spell.''

''We can't do that, Josh,'' Chase said. ''We've been running late all day, and I want to get back to Williamson before dark.''

Mandy took Amelia's hand. ''Come in for just a minute and meet our daughter Emily. She's staying with us a few days, helping me put things in order.''

Mandy introduced the tall, sloe-eyed, delicate-featured woman who was painting the living room. Amelia couldn't see any resemblance to her parents, although now that Mandy was so wrinkled and gray-haired, it was difficult to tell how she would have looked when she was Emily's age.

"This is Emily, our oldest daughter," Mandy said.

Emily stepped off the ladder and shook hands with Amelia and Chase. "We appreciate all you've done for Mom and Daddy."

"They've been a big help to us, too," Amelia said. "In fact, I've been tempted to ask your parents to adopt me."

"They've got big hearts," Emily said, and her gentle laugh was much like her mother's. "They'll be glad to add you to the family."

"Emily brought a lot of pictures to replace the ones we lost," Mandy said, picking up a large photograph of six adults. "We'll hang this one on the wall when she's finished painting. It gives me pleasure to see my kids' faces when I'm doing my housework."

Emily returned to her painting, and Amelia took the picture Mandy held out to her.

"Ain't they a nice family?" Josh said proudly. "Three boys and three girls, not counting the two little tykes who're buried up there on the mountain." He waved an arm toward a cleared area on the mountainside where a few headstones marked a cemetery.

"They are a fine-looking family," Amelia agreed, as she held the framed photograph so Chase could see. Two of the boys looked much like Josh, while the other son and two of the girls had a mixture of their parents' characteristics. Amelia picked out Emily in the photograph, because she had darker features and her body structure was more slender than her siblings.

Jokingly, Amelia said, "With this fine family, you won't want to adopt me."

"There's always room in my heart for one more," Mandy said. "You and Chase are both dear to us already. Just count our place as your home away from home."

"And not that we don't want you to come around," Josh said, "but there's no need to keep bringin' us food. The kids laid in enough groceries to last us for a long time, and Emily's husband fixed our gas stove. We're doin' fine."

Finally, breaking away from the Newberrys' hospitality, Amelia and Chase returned to the ERV.

"Come back and visit us whenever you can," Josh called.

"God go with you," Mandy said.

"They're the most hospitable and unselfish people I've ever known," Amelia said, as she waved to the Newberrys. "Getting to know them has repaid me for the sacrifice I made coming here. Even when I volunteered, I couldn't imagine why I was doing it, but God had some purpose in mind. In the book of James, the writer said that 'faith without works is dead.' The past few days, I've learned a whole new concept about putting my faith into action.''

''Do you think God might have encouraged both of us to come here so we could meet again?'' Chase spoke hesitantly, as if testing the idea, his mind a mixture of hope and anxiety. He walked a very narrow line. If he said too much, he might drive her away, but on the other hand, if he didn't tell Amelia how he felt, she might think he didn't care for her anymore.

Confused, Amelia crossed her arms and looked pointedly away from him. His words had awakened old fears and uncertainties. The silence lengthened between them, making her miserable. Was God speaking to her through Chase's words? Amelia didn't know what to say, so she remained silent.

Only the rumble of the tires on the uneven highway, and the steady hum of the engine, broke the tense silence that surged between them like a heavy fog. A flash of loneliness consumed Amelia. In her mind's eye, she saw a glimpse of paradise, but she had neither the courage nor the wisdom to step inside.

Chapter Eight

Although it was late afternoon when they returned to the church, Rick asked them to make a short run to deliver food to a few families that no one had reached during the day.

Amelia went into the church to give the keys of her Buick to Vicky. She noted that Allen Chambers was standing close to Vicky's desk, and she wondered momentarily if he returned Vicky's obvious affection for him.

"You may be ready to go to the motel before we return," Amelia said to Vicky. "Use my car, and I'll come to the motel with Chase. I don't know how long this trip will take."

"Thanks, Amelia. I'm helping Allen prepare some flyers inviting people to a community worship service Sunday morning. Many church buildings have been flooded and can't be used for a while."

"That sounds like a good idea. And I want to ask my home church in Philadelphia to send Bibles, children's books and any inspirational books. I've learned there's a great need for them."

"You're right, Amelia," Allen Chambers said. "You can have the books sent to Mountainview Church, and our members will distribute them."

"I'll contact my pastor as soon as the phone service is restored."

"And I'll try to send my mother an e-mail and ask her to have a book drive in our church," Vicky said. "I hadn't thought about these people losing their Bibles, too."

Rick and Chase had the ERV loaded when Amelia returned, and they started out again. Amelia was tired, and she could tell by Chase's posture that he was, too. Usually, he stood or sat straight as a poplar tree, but his shoulders slumped forward now. She moved close to him and massaged his neck and shoulders before he started the ERV.

"That feels great. I'd forgotten how soothing a good massage can be."

"I can't get to your left shoulder very well, but this should relax you a little."

They found the isolated hollow, distributed food to the four families living there and started back. They drove mostly in silence, because Chase devoted his attention to the crooked, narrow roads. Numerous mud slides had blocked the roads for several days, and he didn't want to round a curve and plow into a wall of mud and rocks.

He breathed easier when they accessed a paved road going in the direction of town, and he accelerated. But after a few miles, when they went around a sharp curve, Chase braked sharply. A pile of rocks, mud and vegetation had completely covered the road and tumbled down a steep incline toward the river below.

"Oh, Chase," Amelia murmured as she stepped out of the ERV and eyed a huge boulder close to the vehicle. "What are we going to do?"

"I'll have to back up until I find a place to turn around. And that won't be easy, since it's mostly uphill."

"I can walk along beside the vehicle and direct you, if that will help."

"It will, and you can also watch for oncoming traffic."

He adjusted the side mirrors and started backing up slowly, his nerves as taut as a bow string. Trees hung low over the road and occasionally swept the top of the vehicle. Amelia walked beside the slow-moving vehicle, where he could see her and hear any instructions she gave. He backed for a half mile until they reached a spot wide enough to turn the ERV. Fortunately, they hadn't met any other vehicles. When Amelia got back in the car, Chase was wiping perspiration from his face, and his hands were shaking. She poured a cup of coffee for him from the thermos.

He took the cup and gulped the hot brew. "I want to walk around a bit before we go on," he said. "My muscles are tied in knots. How I long for the wide, level roads of the Midwest!"

She realized what a difficult ordeal this had been for him. After her one attempt at driving the ERV, she knew it wasn't easy for him to back the vehicle. After walking for a half hour, she was content to rest in the ERV, but she watched Chase as he tried to loosen his muscles.

Dressed in coveralls that were muddy and wrinkled, Chase didn't look anything like the guy who'd refused to bow to the casual style of his fellow college students. He'd always looked as if he'd just stepped from the pages of a fashion magazine. Yes, the years had made quite a change in Chase Ramsey, and from Amelia's point of view, the changes were all for the better.

Amelia glanced warily at a dark cloud obscuring the sun, hoping more rain wasn't eminent. Chase smiled encouragingly at her when he returned to the vehicle. "We'll have to hurry. I don't want to be caught on this road after dark."

Conscious of the river on her left and the unstable terrain to the right, Amelia was eager to return to town. Because of the narrow road and the possibility of more slides, Chase didn't dare drive too quickly. When, after a few miles, a mud slide blocked the road several feet in front of them, Amelia reached for Chase's hand. He gripped hers tightly.

"This means we can't travel either way," she whispered.

"That's true. We can't go backward or forward. I suppose we could abandon the ERV, climb the mountain and get around the slide, but we'd still have ten miles or more back to Williamson."

He stepped out of the vehicle and looked around. When Amelia joined him, he said, "I don't know enough about mountains to know where a slide is likely to occur. It doesn't seem as if the solid, rock cliffs are slipping. Back a mile or so, there's a sheer rock wall that seemed fairly stable. I might be able to turn the vehicle there, and we can drive that far and plan to spend the night."

"I don't know what else we can do."

"Before it gets completely dark, I'll climb the mountain and see if I can get a signal on my cell phone."

"Be careful," Amelia said.

She watched Chase slip and slide as he climbed the mountain, wondering what he'd do if that particular section of land started shifting. She paced back and forth on the road, and a wave of apprehension unnerved her. Her body trembled when she considered the possibility of being buried in such a slide.

Shaking herself mentally, Amelia said aloud, "Stop it!" Her fears were inconsistent with her faith. God, who had the power to sustain His people every day, also had the power to rescue them from death. And even if death came, that was only a stepping stone from earth to heaven. Trying to recall a Scripture to still her fears, she remembered the closing verse of the twenty-third Psalm. Aloud, she prayed those words to increase her courage.

"'Surely goodness and mercy will follow me all the days of my life, and I will dwell in the house of the Lord forever.'"

"Forever" included not only the here and now, but also the life to come. As her tension decreased, Amelia heard a vehicle on the other side of the rock slide. She rushed in that direction, repeatedly calling for help. No one answered until after she'd shouted several times.

"Who's over there?" a male voice answered.

"Red Cross volunteers. We're stranded between two mud slides. Can you help us?"

"Ma'am, looks like it will take heavy equipment to clear this road. I'm on a motorcycle, and if you want to climb over the slide, I can take you to town on the back of my bike. But it might be risky to get on the slide—looks to me like it's still moving."

Amelia wanted very much to get away from this

area, but she wouldn't leave Chase behind. While she was deliberating, he appeared behind her and she rushed toward him. He put his arm around her.

"Any luck?" she said.

He shook his head, and she explained about the cyclist on the other side of the slide.

"You go with him," Chase urged. "I'll help you over the slide. You'll get muddy, but you can report our predicament and spend the night in comfort."

"I won't leave you alone. Besides, I don't know what kind of person he is."

Since Chase didn't want to be separated from Amelia, either, he shouted to the man. "We'll be safe enough here tonight, but will you notify Rick Smith at Mountainview Church? Tell him that Chase and Amelia are stranded. He'll be worried about us if we don't show up on schedule."

"Okay, buddy. I'll see to it," the man assured them. "Take care tonight."

A feeling of desperation spread through Amelia as she heard the motorcyle departing. She was uncomfortable spending the night with Chase, but she knew, if she had to be stranded, there wasn't anyone else on earth she'd rather have for a companion.

Surveying the mountainside again, Chase said, "The trees are sparse here. There might be another landslide. I'm going to try to turn us around here."

Darkness was complete by the time Chase maneuvered the vehicle into an area beside a sheer rock cliff that looked as if it hadn't changed for centuries and had no notion of going anywhere. He feared for Amelia's safety, but he couldn't find any better protection.

Amelia had walked ahead of him to give any help he needed. He turned off the engine, and she got inside the vehicle.

"Is there any food left?" he asked.

"Enough, I'm sure," Amelia said. "It should still be warm."

She rummaged in her tote bag for a flashlight, and he held it while she ladled food from the insulated containers and put it in two containers. They opened the rear doors of the vehicle and sat on its floor to eat, with their legs dangling above the ground. The overhead lights of the ERV provided limited light. As soon as they finished, Chase said, "We'll have to close the doors so the light won't weaken the battery."

Amelia had heard of darkness so thick it could be cut with a knife, and darkness so dense you couldn't see your hand in front of your eyes. It wasn't *that* dark, but the blackness was oppressive, like a heavy shroud pressing down on her shoulders. She leaned against the ERV, hesitant to move away from its shelter.

Holding the flashlight, Chase scanned the interior of the ERV. "There's room for one of us to sleep on the floor. The other one can curl up on the co-pilot's seat. Take your choice.''

''It doesn't matter. I doubt I'll sleep much any-way,'' Amelia answered. ''How long do you think we'll be here?''

He leaned against the vehicle, and his shoulder touched hers, giving her a greater sense of security. ''Just overnight, I'd imagine. If that cyclist passes the word so Rick knows where we are, he'll have a utility crew out here as soon as possible.''

''But there are so many roads to clear, and the crews are already overworked.'' Her voice was muf-fled, as if a hand had closed around her throat.

Chase realized that Amelia was terrified, and he wanted to gather her into his arms and hold her snugly, but he was uncertain of how she would react to his embrace. It was going to be a long night any-way, and if he angered Amelia, it would be miser-able having to spend the night in the vehicle with her when she was out of sorts. He resisted the im-pulse.

''I wish I could have spared you this,'' he said. ''You aren't used to this kind of work. You should have told Rick you wanted to stay in the office. Then you'd have been safe tonight.''

She would have been safe, but she would have been worried about Chase. If she had her choice, she'd have chosen to be with him. The thought an-noyed her considerably. Amelia didn't want any kind thoughts of Chase. He'd ruined his opportunity to have her think favorably about him. *But that was fifteen years ago,* her conscience needled her. *Are you going to hold a grudge forever?* Up until that minute, she hadn't considered how un-Christian it was for her to continue making Chase pay for what he'd done.

"I'll sleep on the floor that way you can sleep in the copilot's seat rather than under the steering wheel." With the aid of her flashlight, she reached for the bag containing the blankets. "These will come in handy tonight." She handed a blanket to him.

"All right." He took the blanket and moved to the front seat. She wrapped herself in another blanket and lay on the hard floor.

"Do you want the other blanket?" Chase asked.

"I'm all right now, but it may be cold later on. I'm still wearing my heavy clothes, and while I was too hot this afternoon, I'm comfortable now."

She turned off the flashlight, and they settled for sleep, but Amelia was as conscious of his presence as if she'd been in his arms. When the moon spilled a soft radiance into the glade, she looked at her watch and saw that it was only ten o'clock. She folded the extra blanket under her head and closed her eyes, dreading the long hours until daylight.

Amelia's ankle started itching, so she unwound the blanket and scratched her leg. Then her nose began to twitch, and she smothered a sneeze. There must have been dust on the floor near her head. She wasn't completely successful in stopping the sneeze, but she held her nose so only a quiet snort escaped her lips. The sneeze made her nose run, and when sniffing didn't take care of the problem, she wiggled around until she could reach in her jeans pocket for a tissue. She blew daintily, so she wouldn't awaken Chase. She turned from side to side, but she couldn't find a comfortable position. She finally sat up, propped her back against the wall of the vehicle and opened her eyes. She glanced at Chase who had his head pillowed on his arms, which he'd folded on the steering wheel.

"Are you sleeping?" she whispered.

"No," he said immediately, and lifted his head, "but I thought you were. My body is tired, but my mind won't rest."

Conversation about the years they'd been married wasn't a safe subject, so Amelia finally said, "I was surprised to learn that you'd been in the military. When did that happen?"

Chase turned in the seat to face her, but in the dim moonlight, his features were obscure.

"After our breakup I wanted a change of scenery. You probably remember my friend, who was an army recruitment officer. He'd been divorced, so he knew what I was going through. The army needed recruits for people with my computer skills, and he talked me into enlisting. I liked it well enough, but after four years I was ready for civilian life again.''

''Were you in combat?''

''No. I was stationed in Germany most of the time. During my time off, I traveled throughout Europe. It was good for me to be away from home just then. I made new friends to replace the mutual friends we'd had. You've probably learned that a single divorced person is often a liability in many social circles.''

While he talked about his travel experiences, Amelia relaxed to the deep, gentle sound of his voice, and when she yawned several times, Chase said, ''Are you sleepy now?''

''Yes, I think I can go to sleep. Thanks for talking to me.''

And she did go to sleep, only to awaken suddenly when the ERV shook. She heard a thunderous rumble, and a crash that sounded like an explosion. Amelia unwound the blanket and sat upright.

''What is it?'' she cried.

Chase lowered the window to listen. ''Another mud slide, I think. But it's behind us.''

The rude awakening was the last straw, shattering Amelia's composure, and she started crying. ''Chase, I'm scared. What if this whole mountain slides into the river?''

He left the seat and moved to sit beside her. Not knowing whether he dared, he put his arms around

Amelia and she nestled close to him. Caressing her hair, he whispered, "Don't be upset. I'm sure we're safe enough."

"But that big rock above us will crush this ERV if it falls," she said, wiping her eyes with the back of her hand.

"I don't know any other place to go. We're probably as safe in the ERV as we'd be anywhere."

She scooted away from him. "Sorry to be acting like a baby. That doesn't make it any easier for you. I'd just gotten to sleep, and I'm always afraid if I'm awakened suddenly."

"I remember," he said quietly, and smothering a sigh, he moved several feet from her.

Amelia didn't know if it was from fear or cold, but when she shivered, she wrapped the blanket around her again.

"It's getting cold in here." She turned on a flashlight and peered at her watch. "Two o'clock. It's still a long time until daylight. I hope I can go back to sleep."

Chase pulled the blanket off the seat and draped it over his shoulders. "I'll sit here until you go to sleep," he said. "Try not to worry. God looks after His own. There's a promise in the Bible that brings a lot of comfort to me when I'm in a tight place. It's from the seventy-fifth Psalm. 'When the earth and all its people quake, it is I who holds its pillars firm.'"

The Scripture verse did calm Amelia's worries and brought assurance that God would keep them through the night. But the tomblike silence distressed her. Having lived in cities all of her life, Amelia couldn't remember that she'd ever experienced such oppressive quietness. She felt as if she could hear her own heartbeat.

Although she wanted desperately to go to sleep and forget about their predicament, with Chase close enough that she could reach out and touch him, Amelia was still restless. She was overwhelmed with thoughts of the past. Remembering the years she'd shared with Chase, she knew the positive events of their marriage had outweighed the negative. Why had she allowed a few bitter months to erase all the happiness they'd had together?

She sensed tension in the air, and she knew that Chase was also awake. Was he reading her thoughts? At one time they'd been on the same wavelength, able to communicate through their senses as well as with words.

Amelia squirmed, trying to find a comfortable position. It was a long time before either of them went to sleep.

Chapter Nine

A shaft of moonlight illuminated the vehicle when Amelia awakened. She felt drowsily content, until she realized that she and Chase lay side by side, with her head on his shoulder. He had his arm around her, his head resting on hers. His breath was warm against her ear and his even heartbeat throbbed steadily against her side. Drowsy as she was, Amelia realized that she experienced a contentment she hadn't known for years. She stirred, and his arms tightened, holding her in place.

"Melly," he whispered, and Amelia gasped. That's what he'd called her during their most intimate moments. His dreams must have been the same as hers had been.

Trembling, Amelia carefully backed out of Chase's embrace, hoping he was unaware of their closeness. He groaned slightly and reached for her, but his soft breathing continued, and he didn't awaken. Apparently, she'd snuggled close to him in her sleep and, instinctively, he'd gathered her into his arms, as he'd always done when she got cold in the night.

Reveling in the comfort of awakening in Chase's arms, Amelia wondered if, by her stubbornness, she'd wasted fifteen years. Up until that episode with Rosemary, she and Chase had been happy. Had she been wrong to allow a few transgressions on Chase's part to separate them?

Amelia inched slowly away from Chase until she was on the opposite end of the ERV. She intended to feign sleep when he awakened, but while he slept, she watched him closely, taking in every single detail of his face revealed in the soft moonlight. His mouth curved tenderly, and a hint of a smile hovered on his lips. He turned his head toward her, and his lips parted in a long, exhausted sigh. Yesterday's driving had been difficult for him, and she knew he was still tired.

Amelia's thoughts trickled back to the day she'd met Chase. She'd been lonely that day because she'd learned that her parents were going to Hawaii, without having invited her to join them. Even when she was a child, they'd never taken her on vacation with them. She was shipped off to one of her grandmothers when her parents wanted to go someplace.

When Amelia was in her midteens, they willingly paid for her to take tours with her friends, so she'd traveled to many places, but it always rankled that her parents didn't need or want her company. She should have been used to it by the time she was in college, but she couldn't understand why they didn't treat her the way other parents treated their children. Most parents with only one child tended to be possessive, but not her mother and father.

On the day she'd met Chase, she'd been walking with her head down thinking about her parents' lack of devotion. She'd bumped headlong into Chase as he came out of the college library. She'd knocked him off stride, and his books had fallen from his hands. She stooped down to pick them up, while at the same time apologizing for her clumsiness.

He'd knelt to help her retrieve the books and had brushed away her apologies. He invited her to go with him to the student center for a soda before their next classes. Before they parted, he'd asked her for a date. She didn't accept, but he gave her his telephone number. Although she'd thought about him often, she hadn't called him. Two weeks later, she met him at a birthday event for all students having birthdays during the month of June. Not only had Chase and she been born in the same month, but on the same day and in the same year. This mutual birthday seemed to tie them together, and they started dating steadily.

They were married a year later, and they'd gone to Hawaii on their honeymoon. Sensing her down-heartedness over her parents' neglect, Chase had tried to make up for that inattention by taking her anyplace she wanted to go. Her lips softened as she recalled the days of laughter they'd enjoyed.

To shift her thoughts from unbidden territory, Amelia watched as daylight filtered around the vehicle. Through the lowered window, she inhaled deeply of the fresh mountain air, thrilling to the clear, sweet song of a cardinal perched on a tree limb overhanging the roadway. Chase shivered and pulled the blanket closer around his shoulders, and she stepped across him to close the window.

When Chase awakened, Amelia was sitting in the copilot's seat. Yawning sleepily, he opened his eyes slightly.

"What time is it?" he asked.

"Seven o'clock," she said.

"I wonder what we should do now."

"Is there anything we can do until someone comes to clear the road? The two of us couldn't move all of that mud, even if we had a shovel."

He sat up, rubbed his eyes and ran his fingers through his wavy hair. "I figure Rick will get someone to us as soon as possible, but there are hundreds of roads like this, and a limited amount of equipment to do the work."

Apparently, he hadn't been aware of their close

embrace in the night. Amelia was relieved that she didn't have to deal with any discussion about it.

"We might have breakfast," she suggested.

"I'm not up for meat loaf and cold mashed potatoes this time of day, but we can eat fruit and bread."

By the time they'd finished eating, the sun had peeked over the high mountain to the east.

Since there was still no sign of a rescue party, Chase suggested, "Let's walk awhile. My muscles are tight from sleeping in the vehicle, and I need some exercise. We'll hear when the machinery comes to remove the landslide."

He took her hand, and she laced his fingers with her own. They walked companionably, looking at the wildflowers growing along the road, most of which they couldn't name, but they admired them. There were bell-shaped, funnel-like flowers of five points, light violet in color on slender stems. Another plant had loose clusters of purple tubular flowers with a spreading lip. Of course, they recognized the dandelions.

"Dandelions are pretty here in the countryside," Chase said, "and I admire their hardiness, but they're not welcome in my lawn."

"You live in a house rather than an apartment?"

"A small one in the town of Worthington, an historic town surrounded by the big city of Columbus.

I like to putter around in a yard when I have the time, so I don't want to live in an apartment."

"I remember the flower gardens you had at our home in Kansas. I liked the bouquets you arranged from your own flowers more than the ones you bought for me at the florist."

Their clasped hands tightened, and they walked in silence for several minutes, remembering happier days.

"I live in a three-room apartment, which is big enough for me," she said. "I rarely have any company."

Comparing her life in Philadelphia to the quiet peace of this morning, Amelia was thankful that they'd been marooned for the night. These hours together had brought a meaningful perspective to their new relationship. She sensed that Chase and she would never be completely separated again.

"This morning reminds me of the day I became a Christian," Chase said. "Although he didn't pressure me, Wesley, my best friend in the army, always invited me to go to chapel with him. I refused until one Easter morning when we were in Germany. He asked me to go with him to a sunrise service on a mountain near Frankfurt conducted by our army chaplain. For some reason I couldn't understand at the time, I wanted to go with him. I know now that the Holy Spirit was prompting me to go." He looked directly at Amelia. "Do you understand what I mean?"

"Yes, because I've had similar experiences." She recalled vividly the conviction that it was God's will for her to volunteer to come to West Virginia.

"I'd been aware that there was something 'different' about Wesley," Chase continued. "No matter where we were, he'd pray silently before he ate. He got a lot of ribbing about it from our buddies, but he'd just smile and go on eating his food as if he hadn't heard them. You could count on him to be the first to offer help if anyone needed it. He was a good soldier and obeyed orders without complaint."

"In other words, he exemplified the teachings of Jesus."

"That's right. It hurt my conscience when he went to chapel alone, time after time. So when he asked me to attend the Easter service, I decided to go and persuaded a few other guys to go with us."

Lost in his memories of that morning, Chase stopped walking and leaned against a maple tree beside the road. Unconsciously, he put his arm around Amelia, drawing her into a light embrace. As he looked through the trees toward the flooded Tug Fork Valley, he continued. "It was a beautiful place, with hundreds of people gathered, and for the first time in my life, I understood the meaning of Easter. The chaplain didn't talk more than fifteen minutes, but it was the greatest moment of my life. I felt as if the message was for me alone. That was a new beginning for me. Wesley acted as my mentor for the next six months, and as soon as I was discharged, I found a church home. I've been serving the Lord since then.''

Chase had been wanting to share his conversion experience, and subsequent spiritual journey, with Amelia since they'd first bumped into each other again. He knew that any further relationship they had must be founded upon the Lordship of Jesus. There had been a void in his life after his separation from Amelia. He'd believed that his service to the Lord had filled that void, but having seen Amelia again, he knew that part of the emptiness in his life had been provoked by his need for her. He tightened the embrace and Amelia snuggled closer. Was now the time to suggest that they might reunite?

"I'm glad you told me, Chase." Amelia interrupted his thoughts. "It's strange that it took our separation to push us in the right direction spiritually. I was very despondent after our divorce. Our marriage had failed, and my parents obviously didn't want me to live with them. I was on the verge of clinical depression, and my doctor advised me to seek counseling.

"He sent me to a Christian counselor. Like your friend, Wesley, she invited me to go to church with her. I started attending a support group of singles, each of whom had gone through a divorce. One of them helped me get a job with the Red Cross, and I moved away from my parents and relocated in Philadelphia. I slowly got my priorities in order. I haven't lived a very exciting life, but it's been a satisfying one. I'm still a long way from where I want to be spiritually.''

"I understand that. None of us ever reaches spiritual perfection in this life, but it's a goal to keep us moving forward.''

They walked as far as the first slide, and when they turned to go back to the ERV, they heard machinery working ahead of them. They hurried along, but it was almost noon before the bulldozer had cleared one lane of the highway, enabling them to continue their drive to town.

"This mountain is still moving, and there's no guarantee that it won't close the road again,'' the bulldozer operator told them, ''so be careful. You never know when there'll be another mud slide.''

But they returned to Williamson without mishap, and when they reported to Red Cross headquarters, Rick had already sent someone else to make their food deliveries.

"Go to the motel and freshen up and take a nap. I don't suppose you had much rest,'' he said.

"We both slept,'' Amelia said, ''but not very well.''

They'd started toward the parking lot, when

Vicky came to the door and called Rick. "There's a call from the state police."

"Hey, you two," she said, coming toward them. "I worried about you all night. I'm so thankful you're back safe and sound." She grinned broadly. "But your clothes look like you slept in them."

"As we did," Amelia responded, laughing. "Has anything new happened that we should know about?"

"Not much. Allen and I delivered about two hundred flyers yesterday about the joint worship service Sunday. He believes it's necessary for the people to be united in worship during this crisis. The service will continue during most of the afternoon, so people can come and go at their convenience."

When Vicky mentioned Allen's name, she was radiant, and Amelia wondered if she was building up sorrow for herself. Allen Chambers appeared to be a man completely focused on his ministry.

"And we've received several boxes of books and Bibles from my church," Vicky said. "Our semi brought another load of supplies that included reading material."

With a harried look on his face, Rick joined them, "We have an emergency call, and no one to take it. A pregnant woman needs to go to the hospital, and the bridge into her town has been washed out. The husband will bring his wife across the backwater in a boat, but I have to find someone to pick her up and bring her to the hospital.''

"I'll go," Chase said.

"Aw, I can't ask you to do that," Rick said. "Maybe I can find someone else. You've had a rough night."

"That doesn't matter. I didn't expect an easy time when I volunteered to help."

"The floodwall gates are open now, so you can bring her to the Williamson hospital, but you may have a few detours in driving to her area. I'll sketch a map for you."

"I'll go, too," Amelia said. "You can drive my car, Chase, and that will give enough space so the husband can ride to the hospital with us, too."

Chase noted the dark streaks under Amelia's eyes, and the weary expression on her face. She'd been restless in her sleep, moaning occasionally as if she were having bad dreams. She hadn't really slept peacefully until he'd gathered her into his arms and cuddled her as he would have a child. She'd sighed softly against his chest and seemed to rest at last, but the hard work of the past few days was taking a toll on her. He wanted to spare her as much as possible.

"No, Amelia. Get some rest. I'll manage."

Knowing the hazards for the volunteers in this disaster area, Amelia would be uneasy until he returned anyway, so she knew she wouldn't sleep.

She shook her head slowly. "No, I want to go with you." There seemed to be a slight emphasis on the word *you,* and Chase took a sharp breath. Their eyes caught and held, and for a poignant moment, the world stood still for them. Momentarily, their differences disappeared. The vows they'd taken to "love, honor and cherish" came to the forefront, and they were one again

His eyes alight with tenderness and caring, Chase stepped toward her, just as Rick, who hadn't observed the emotional exchange between Amelia and Chase, called in the direction of the cooking tent, "Hey, how about fixing up a thermos of coffee and some sandwiches for Amelia and Chase?"

When Rick turned toward them, he flushed, apparently realizing he'd blundered into something he didn't have the right to share. For a moment, he seemed tempted to turn aside, but the difficult moment passed when he said, "I'm sorry to send you out when you haven't had any rest, but this is the woman's first baby, and she's having problems."

Chase glanced quickly at Amelia. She didn't meet his eyes, but he noticed that her fingers balled into knots, and she stuck her hands into her pockets.

"If you'd rather not go, Amelia," he said softly. "I can go alone."

She shook her head. "I'll go—she might need another woman with her." She reached into the ERV and picked up her tote bag and started inside the church. "But give me a few minutes to wash my face and clean my teeth. I'll be back by the time our food is prepared."

Amelia was overwhelmed by that magnetic moment she'd shared with Chase, and she had to be alone for a few minutes to calm her emotions.

"God," she whispered, *"do I love him? Does he still love me? Does love ever die? The old spark between us is alive and well, yet different somehow. What am I going to do?"*

Chapter Ten

When they arrived at the site of the destroyed bridge, a state trooper was helping a pitiful little group of three people up the riverbank. The husband didn't appear to be more than twenty, and his wife looked even younger. The girl wasn't visibly pregnant, and Amelia assumed that she was in the early months of her pregnancy. Amelia's compassion went out to the young woman, and she empathized with the trauma surrounding the couple. An older woman, a resigned look on her face, had an arm around the young woman, who slumped over in pain.

"I'm Jerry Anderson," the young man said as he hurried forward. "My wife's name is Michelle, and her mother is Norma. If you don't have room for all of us, I'll stay behind. Michelle wants her mother with her."

"Of course, she wants her mother," Amelia said, remembering how often she'd longed for her mother when she faced a crisis. "But there's space for all of you. The back seat is roomy."

She opened the rear door, and Jerry took one look at the spotless gray upholstery and carpet.

"Oh, ma'am," he said, "we're so muddy. We'll ruin your car."

"Get in," she urged. "The car can be cleaned, and your wife needs to see a doctor as soon as possible."

Amelia squeezed Michelle's shoulders tenderly as she helped her into the car. Chase was surprised, and pleased, at the efficiency Amelia used in handling the situation. He kept forgetting that Amelia was no longer the insecure young woman he'd married. While he drove, she asked some pertinent questions.

"Has the hospital been notified that you're coming?"

"Yes," Jerry said. "The trooper radioed the hospital."

"How far along is she?" she asked.

"Three months," Norma said. "She's been doing fine, but her home was flooded, and they lost everything. She's been awful nervous and upset about that. She started bleeding this morning. I thought she needed to see a doctor."

"Especially since it's her first baby," Amelia said.

"I'm awful worried about her," Jerry whispered.

Amelia throat constricted, and she sought for words to comfort the couple. She glanced hopelessly at Chase.

"You made the right decision," he said.

"She'll soon be in good hands."

When they reached Williamson, Chase maneuvered the Buick through crowded streets and up the mountain to the four-story hospital. He found a convenient parking space, and he and Jerry helped Michelle up the ramp into the waiting room. Although the hospital must have been pushed to the hilt with emergencies, an aide had a stretcher waiting for them. Clutching her stomach, Michelle was soon whisked into the emergency room.

Before Jerry followed his wife and mother-in-law, he shook hands with Chase and nodded shyly at Amelia.

"We sure do appreciate your help. We'll be okay now, so you won't have to stay."

Amelia looked meaningfully at Chase and shook her head.

Correctly interpreting her mood, he said, "We'll stay until you hear what the doctors have to tell you. We'll be in the waiting room. Let us know."

Amelia chose a seat that was separated from anyone else. She couldn't talk, and she picked up a magazine and started leafing through it. The hospital had emergency phone service, and Chase asked a nurse to call Rick Smith and notify him that they'd arrived at the hospital. She handed him the phone so he could talk to Rick.

Chase explained the situation to Rick, who said, "You've done all you can do. Go get some rest."

"We'll stick around here for a while, then we'll go directly to the motel when we leave the hospital. Call the motel if you need us before morning."

"I won't call you. It's easy to burn out on a volunteer mission like this. People see the widespread need, and push themselves beyond their strength. You two need to get some sleep. I'm sure you didn't get any rest last night."

Chase returned to sit beside Amelia. He respected her mood and turned his attention to a television program, but he couldn't become interested in the world news on CNN. At the moment, he had enough problems of his own. The world turmoil faded into the background as he considered his renewed interest in the woman by his side.

The next hour passed slowly, and Amelia looked often at her watch. Her body longed for rest, but she didn't think she'd be able to sleep until she knew that Michelle was all right. What a terrible ordeal for the young woman! She'd lost her home and now was on the verge of losing her baby.

Although they'd eaten the sandwiches Rick had provided on the way to pick up the Andersons,

Chase decided some more food would ease their fatigue. He went into the hospital's lobby and got two cans of root beer and candy bars from the dispensers, and bought a local newspaper.

Amelia smiled her thanks when he returned with the food, and although she didn't eat the candy, she sipped the cold drink. The room was crowded with people, coming and going, and there wasn't any occasion for private conversation. After they finished the drinks, and he'd disposed of the cans, Chase draped his arm loosely over Amelia's shoulders. She didn't rebuff him as he gently massaged the tense muscles of her neck and shoulders.

They waited two more hours before Jerry came into the room. His morose face told the story before he stammered, with tears in his eyes, "She—she lost the baby."

"I'm so sorry," Amelia whispered, and Chase stood and took Jerry's hand.

"Is Michelle all right?" Chase asked.

Jerry tried to smile. "Yes, except she's awful disappointed. But the doctor told her that she's young and she can have lots of babies—he said to wait a few months and try again."

"I'm sure you will have other children," Chase said, "But that doesn't help much now."

"Is she going to be released?" Amelia asked.

"Not 'til morning. Since she'd have to ride a boat

back home, the doctor will keep her overnight. Norma and I are going to stay with her.''

''We'll be assigned to other duties tomorrow,'' Chase said, ''but if you need transportation, contact the Red Cross center and someone will help you.''

''Thanks a heap,'' Jerry said. ''You've been so good to us.''

Chase gave Jerry a brotherly hug, and they watched him as he hurried back to Michelle.

As they neared her car in the parking lot, Chase took the Buick's keys from his pocket and handed them to Amelia. ''Do you want to drive now?''

She shook her head. Tears trickled from her eyes and down her cheeks. He held the door open for her and went to the driver's seat. What should he do now? As the days had passed, he kept thinking there might be a chance of reconciliation between them, but he couldn't push Amelia. He didn't want to do the wrong thing. Would she rebuff him if he tried to comfort her now? He knew her sadness was for herself as well as for Michelle.

Her tears turned to open sobs, and the sound unnerved him, especially since Amelia wasn't normally a crying woman. Flinging caution aside, and not caring who might see them, Chase crowded into the large bucket seat beside Amelia. With tears misting his own eyes, he put his arm around her shaking shoulders. When she turned toward him, he gathered her into a tight embrace on his lap. Her arms went around his waist, and she clung fiercely to him. He pulled her head to his shoulders, and his fingers caressingly threaded through her soft hair.

"Cry it out, Melly," he whispered.

After a while, when she quieted, he said, "I'm sorry you're still sad about losing our baby, but I guess the years never erase some memories. All evening, I've thought about the night I sat in the waiting room when you miscarried. I knew you were remembering, too."

She wiped her face on the collar of his shirt. "I thought I'd moved past losing the baby, but helping Michelle brought back my pain and disappointment. And until this minute, I didn't realize that you were hurting as much as I was over losing the baby. I drew into my own shell for a while and didn't see that you needed me. Was that the reason you turned to Rosemary?"

Chase was stunned into silence, but he breathed a silent, *Thank you, God.* When the news had circulated in their town about his affair with Rosemary, he'd tried to talk to Amelia, tried to tell her that it wasn't anything he'd planned, and she absolutely wouldn't listen to him. Now it seemed she was ready to talk.

Before he could formulate an answer, Amelia continued. "I know some men don't want women who can't give them children. I thought that might have been your reason for seeking out someone else.''

''That isn't true. I've no doubt we could have had other children. You heard what Jerry said—the doctor told them to wait awhile and try again.''

''I wanted our baby more than anything I'd ever wanted in my life. It was something I could do myself, not something my parents gave me. When you and I separated, I gave up my dreams, but I've always wanted a child of my own.''

''Many women in their forties have children now.'' He wanted to add, ''If we remarry, there's still time,'' but her next words put an end to that line of thought.

She shook her head. ''But *I* can't. I developed fibroid tumors and had to have a complete hysterectomy five years ago.''

''Your miscarriage didn't have anything to do with Rosemary. I was sorry we lost the baby, but that didn't change my love for you. Although it might have looked that way to you, I didn't pursue Rosemary. I'd dated her before I met you, but I didn't love her.''

''She kept trying to break us up.''

''Which didn't affect me at all. I had no interest in Rosemary, and I was only slightly annoyed when she came to work where I did. She kept approaching me, but that night we had to stay out of town, and you wouldn't answer the phone, my defenses were down. I was so ashamed of myself—I was determined that it wouldn't happen again.''

"But you kept seeing her."

"Yes. You wouldn't let me talk about it. When you acted as if you didn't even care, I childishly thought that if I was going to be blamed for something, I might as well do what I was blamed for. I saw Rosemary a few times, but I'd broken up with her before we got a divorce. I haven't seen her since."

"Has there been anyone else?" Amelia asked, knowing she had no right to pry into his relationships.

"I haven't been intimate with anyone, if that's what you mean. But I liked being married and having a home, so I wanted to get married again. I've dated several women, but I've always stopped short of proposing."

Amelia pulled out of Chase's arms and leaned her head against the back of the seat. She sighed and gripped his hand.

"Looks like we made a mess of our lives, didn't we?" she said.

"I'll have to take the blame."

"No, Chase. I should have been more understanding and met you halfway. But my pride was hurt—first losing the baby, and then losing my husband, too. I thought divorce was the only way, but a year passed before I could live a normal life. My parents didn't have time for me, I'd moved away and left our friends, and I'd lost you. As I told you this morning, my life didn't take on new meaning until I became a Christian.''

''But are you happy now?'' Chase said.

''Happiness is hard to define, isn't it? I'm content with my life, but that isn't necessarily happiness.'' Amelia yawned. ''We should go now. I'm sorry I've kept you, but it seemed as if Michelle's trauma became mine. I lost my composure.''

Chase was tired, but he didn't want to leave matters between Amelia and him so unsettled. He'd waited years to explain what had happened between him and Rosemary, and he was elated that she seemed to understand why he'd strayed.

He cupped Amelia's face with his hands and turned her head until he could look into her eyes. ''But what about now, Melly? We can't change what happened before, but perhaps God is giving us another opportunity.'' Timorously, he whispered, ''Are you interested in trying again?''

''I don't know. If you'd asked that question a week ago, my answer would have been an unequivocal no. Now I'm not so sure, and I'm too bushed to give you an answer now.''

Her answer halfway encouraged Chase, and with a lighter heart, he drove to the motel.

''After we've rested, let's have dinner together. We haven't had much to eat today.''

"I'd like that," she agreed.

He walked with Amelia to her room on the second floor. Before she inserted the key in the door, she looked up at him expectantly. He brushed her lips slowly with his.

"Sleep well, Melly," he said, and turned quickly away.

Chase entered his room musing on some private memories. He was eager to be married to Amelia again, but he had to put bounds to his desires. Amelia's guard had slipped a little, but he wasn't sure she'd completely forgiven him.

He was troubled to learn about Amelia's hysterectomy. She would have made a wonderful mother. The news had shattered his dreams, too. Because of her unhappiness, Chase hadn't let Amelia know how unhappy he'd been when they'd lost their baby. He had several nieces and nephews, and without a child of his own, he always felt left out during family gatherings. But if Amelia couldn't be the mother of his child, he no longer wanted one.

When Amelia entered the sanctuary of Mountainview Church with Vicky on Sunday afternoon, she was gratified to see that the room was filled. Chase and Rick were serving as ushers and Chase directed them to two empty seats on the right side of the room. Allen gave a stirring message of hope, and Amelia watched the expressions of the people, many of which changed from despair to hope as Allen preached and prayed.

Several gospel-singing groups from the tri-state area of West Virginia, Kentucky and Virginia had volunteered their time and talent for a concert. An offering was taken during the service to aid the flood victims.

The boxes of used and new books and Bibles that had been received from Amelia's church, as well as from the church where Vicky and Chase attended, had been arranged on tables in the foyer of the church. Each family was given a Bible. Books for adults and books for children were placed on separate tables. Each person attending would go home with at least one book.

At the end of the service, with a beaming smile, Allen said, "And now I have a surprise for you. During the two years that I've been your pastor, I've been urged by young and old alike to get married. In fact, I've had enough potential brides suggested to me that I could have acquired a harem if I so desired."

He paused until the roar of laughter, spawned by his remark, subsided. "While I appreciated all your efforts, I really wanted to make the decision myself. And, today, I'm going to introduce you to my future bride, who will soon be serving with me as my wife."

Vicky gasped, and Amelia turned to her. Vicky's

face was a mottled red and white. Her breath came in gasps.

"Do you suppose he's going to propose to me before all these people?" she whispered.

Amelia was distressed that Vicky had jumped to this conclusion, since Amelia hadn't noticed that Allen had shared Vicky's romantic notions. She wasn't surprised when Allen beckoned to someone in the front row.

"Will you come up now, Patsy?"

A young, petite brunette walked gracefully up the steps to the platform, and she turned to the congregation with a fetching smile. Allen put his arm around her waist.

"Since most of my friends and neighbors are present today, I wanted to take this opportunity to introduce my fiancée, Patsy Chapman. Patsy and I have been engaged for two years, but we waited until she finished her seminary training before we announced our wedding plans. Patsy has a degree in Christian Education, and I'm looking forward to having her join my ministry."

Under the cover of the congregation's standing round of applause, Amelia took Vicky by the arm and led her up the side aisle. She darted out the first door she saw, which opened on the parking lot, pulling her stunned companion behind her. Vicky didn't speak until they reached Amelia's car.

Covering her face, Vicky said, "Oh, how stupid

I've been. He didn't care for me at all. I can't face him again. I want to go home.''

''Are you prepared to explain to your parents why you're coming home early?'' Amelia said as she drove away from the church.

''No. They'd never understand. And I won't run out on a commitment, but I can't see him again.''

''I'm sure Rick will find other work for you. Tell him that you want to work out in the field. I imagine that your office work is less demanding now.''

''Yes, that's true. But I'm so upset.''

Amelia wondered if Vicky's distress was generated more from embarrassment rather than unrequited love. But since she hadn't done so well with her own love life, she didn't feel qualified to advise Vicky.

''I suppose it's easy to tell you that you'll get over it, that you'll forget Allen, and you probably will. You're only eighteen, and your emotions are still volatile. Even if you do love him, people love more than once. When people lose their mates through divorce or death, they often marry again, and they say they've loved both spouses.''

''But I was so sure that marriage to a preacher was God's will for my life,'' Vicky moaned.

''It still might be, but that preacher must not be Allen. Just remember I'm here to listen, Vicky. Don't bottle up your troubles. Talk to me about them.''

Chapter Eleven

The next few days were so busy that Chase and Amelia had little time to discuss renewing their relationship. When Vicky told Rick that she wanted to work in the field, he assigned Amelia to drive an ERV into easily accessed places and asked Vicky to be her copilot. Chase and Amelia had little opportunity to say more than a greeting on passing. Amelia thought it might be for the best, although she missed Chase and wanted to be with him.

Chase was assigned to go into an isolated community, accessible only by motorboat, and as he traveled, he was conscious of the fact that only a week was left of the time he and Amelia had committed to spend in the disaster area. Of course, they could stay on because the cleanup effort would go on for months, but most of Chase's vacation time was gone, and he knew Amelia needed to return soon to her office work in Philadelphia. She'd mentioned some pending reports that a volunteer couldn't do.

So when a group of the Red Cross workers made plans during the evening hours, both of them gladly agreed to help to make Willie Honaker's home livable. Willie had refused to apply for a mobile home, and a few of the volunteers were carpenters who thought they could salvage his house. A church in Williamson pledged to pay for the renovations.

The local residents had repaired the road enough that cars and pickups could drive into the hollow, but given the widespread destruction in the county, it might be years before a road would be ready for all traffic. Willie's house has been torn in two, but the elderly man was content to stay in the half house. The workers shored up the foundation of the part that contained the kitchen, a living room and an upstairs bedroom. They put new siding and a roof on the house.

Chase couldn't believe that the Amelia he'd been married to for five years would climb to the roof of the house and crawl around on bruised knees to help attach shingles. At the end of one particularly hot day, which had been full from seven o'clock in the morning until dusk, Chase looked at Amelia as she splashed water over her face and hands from a bucket of water pumped from Willie's now cleaned and purified water supply.

Spots of tar blotched her skin. Scarred, reddened knees peeped through holes in her jeans. Her hair was dirty and it hung in disarray around her face. But when they got in his truck to start back to the motel, her eyes were serene and calm, and a soft smile played around her lips.

"Been quite a day, hasn't it?" she said, and she sighed as she settled into the seat. She pulled down the visor and looked at herself in the mirror.

"Oh!" she screeched. She glanced at Chase. "Why don't you look as bedraggled as I do?"

"Maybe you worked harder than I did," he said, tossing a enigmatic grin in her direction.

Before he started the engine, Chase took his billfold from his hip pocket and removed a photo of Amelia that had been taken soon after their marriage. His mouth curved into an unconscious smile when he looked at this image of Amelia, the same one he'd always carried in his mind.

Velvety dark eyes with long, curling lashes were the outstanding features of a near-perfect delicate face, marred only by a deep dimple near the corner of her full red mouth. Dark hair flowed over her proud shoulders.

"Do you want to make a comparison?" he said.

Amelia looked at the photo, then glanced in the mirror again.

"Meanie! It's not nice to show me how much I've changed," she rebuked teasingly to cover her inner tumult.

The change in her appearance was astonishing, but the thing that amazed Amelia most wasn't that, compared to her former self, she looked like a slob today. The big surprise was that Chase still carried her picture. Immediately after their divorce, she'd boxed away all of the photos of Chase and every other picture that reminded her of their life together. She hadn't looked at them since.

Chase turned her face toward him, and in spite of the dirt and sweat, he kissed her cheek.

"To me, you're more beautiful right now than you were when this picture was taken. The photo shows only the outward appearance, but when I look at you now, I know what you're like on the inside. The true Amelia Stone shows through."

Her hand lifted to cradle his chin. "Thanks."

As they drove out of the hollow, Amelia said, "My three weeks will be finished next Wednesday. I feel guilty to leave so much work undone here, but I do have a commitment to my job."

"And my leave of absence is up next week, too. Have you thought any more about *us?*" he asked hesitantly.

"Yes, I have. But I can't see anything except obstacles to our reconciliation. For one thing, your parents wouldn't be pleased. I overheard your mother tell you once that you'd be better off without me.''

A look of distaste spread across Chase's face. ''And if you remember, I didn't agree with her. But regardless, I'm in my forties now—I make my own decisions. If I please my parents, well and good, but that won't influence my decision. They need to change their attitudes.''

''I was never sure what they had against me.''

''Oh, it wasn't you. They didn't like your parents because Dad and your father belonged to different political parties. They'd been involved in several verbal disagreements over their favorite political candidates. Dad isn't active in politics now, so I don't think what we do will matter so much.''

Amelia didn't mention what she most feared. Would she ever be able to forget that Chase had betrayed her with Rosemary? Anybody but Rosemary! Her rival wasn't very attractive, and she had an acid personality. That Chase would reject her for a girl like Rosemary had rankled more than anything else, although she had thought that time had changed her attitude about that. After seeing Chase again, she wasn't sure.

Amelia believed his story that Rosemary had been the instigator of their affair, because that was the kind of thing Rosemary would do. Amelia supposed she was being foolish, but she still couldn't stand the thought of sharing Chase with some other woman. She admitted that their divorce had been a mistake, but it might be another mistake if she went back to Chase before she knew for sure that she was ready to let go of the past.

When he'd broken his wedding vows, neither Chase nor she were Christians. Now that God had forgiven her of her sins, wasn't she mature enough to completely forgive Chase for his transgressions? The Bible taught that she should. "If your brother sins, rebuke him, and if he repents, forgive him."

Chase was her husband, but he was also her Christian brother. The words of the Bible were plain enough for anyone to understand. Chase had repented. She believed that he was truly sorry for what he'd done; therefore, she should forgive him. Her heart prompted her to start over, but could she ever *forget* his infidelity? Until his actions no longer bothered her, she couldn't give Chase any encouragement.

"I don't know what to tell you," she said. "I've been comfortable with you as I used to be, and I don't feel any animosity toward you. A month ago, I wouldn't have believed that was possible. I'd prayed to have the grace to forgive any heartache you'd caused me, but I still couldn't forget what had happened. But most of the time since we've been reunited, I don't even think about Rosemary. I've been contented to be with you again, sharing the same things."

"That's a beginning. It may be that we'll have to start over, as if we've never been together."

"Our days are so full that I usually fall asleep as soon as my head hits the pillow. I'm not used to getting up at six o'clock and working ten hours a day. I don't have time to think. I may not know what to do by the time we leave this area."

"Philadelphia and Columbus aren't far away by plane. Promise me that you won't disappear again and shut me out completely."

"I promise," she said, and she traced the contour of his face with her fingers. "We may have to be only friends, but I don't want you to go out of my life."

"Being friends is better than nothing," Chase said, but in his heart, he knew that wasn't enough for him.

Amelia sat up suddenly, wondering at the strange sound. Vicky was struggling awake in the other bed.

"What is that?" she asked when she saw Amelia stirring.

A steady roar sounded throughout the room, and streaks of lightning pierced the darkness. Amelia stepped out of bed and went to the window.

"It's raining!" she said, awestruck at the amount of water blowing against the windows and splashing on the ground below. Vicky ran to her side.

"Raining!" Vicky said. "And just when the river

was finally below flood stage. I've never seen it rain this hard.''

''Neither have I.''

''I've heard of 'raining cats and dogs,' which never did make any sense to me. Maybe that's what's happening now.''

Amelia went back to her bed and looked at her watch. Three o'clock. ''If this continues very long, those hollows will be flooded again. Let's pray that no one will perish, that they'll have time to take shelter on higher ground.''

''I don't know why people build in those little hollows,'' Vicky complained, ''when they know there will be floods.''

Amelia smiled, for the thought had crossed her mind more than once. ''Spoken like a true Midwesterner,'' she said. ''Families who've lived in these hollows for generations aren't going to move. Besides, where else could they build homes in this mountainous area? Ohio has tornadoes. Do people leave just because they think a tornado might come? Floridians know they'll likely have hurricanes, but they continue to live there. Humans always have the feeling, when a disaster occurs, that it won't happen again. They try to put their lives back in order, believing the future will be better than the past.''

Should she take the same attitude toward a new marriage with Chase? She was sure he wanted them to marry again. When she took the vow, '''til death do us part," she believed those words put a seal on their future. If God had joined them together, did the divorce really do away with their marriage, or were they still man and wife?

She knew that Christians sometimes lost fellowship with God, but reconciliation was always available and waiting. Just because a person made a mistake, even many mistakes, that wasn't any reason to believe that God no longer loved that individual. When someone asked forgiveness with an honest and contrite heart, as the Scriptures said, God was always ready to forgive. Perhaps she should follow that policy in her feelings about Chase.

Amelia couldn't go back to sleep. Her concern for the local residents, who'd likely be involved in a flash flood, and the dilemma of how to approach a new relationship with Chase churned in her head. The rain didn't lessen all night. When the alarm went off at six o'clock, she was glad to get out of bed, but she wondered what the day would bring.

Chase knew what time she awakened, and when her phone rang, she was sure he was calling.

"Good morning," she said into the receiver.

"I'm not so sure," he answered grimly. "Have you heard the weather forecast?"

"No. We haven't turned on the television."

"At least four inches of rain is predicted for the West Virginia coalfields today. That's almost as much as caused the flood last month."

"What can we do?"

"Get dressed quickly and go to the service center at the church. I've been talking with Rick, and he doesn't think we can deliver much food today, but there'll be plenty for us to do. I'm ready to leave now."

"Vicky and I are awake, so we'll see you soon."

During their marriage, when Chase and she had ended a phone conversation, she'd always said, "Love you." Her lips trembled on those words now, but she hung up without saying them. Was her subconscious telling her the desire of her heart? In spite of her effort to block him from her mind, did she still love Chase? It was a disturbing, yet at the same time, an exciting thought.

Amelia became aware that Vicky was staring at her and that she was sitting on the bed staring into space.

Her face colored, and she stammered, "D-did you say something?"

"I asked you what Mr. Ramsey had told you, but forget that and answer another question. What's between you and Mr. Ramsey anyway? All of us have noticed some kind of spark between you. You must have been more than casual friends in the past. Were you sweethearts?"

Amused at the old-fashioned term, Amelia smiled. "Yes. I guess we were." To forestall more questioning, she said, "I'll shower quickly, so you can take your turn. We need to get over to the church quickly. They need us."

As Rick made the daily assignments, he said, "I'm undecided about taking our food runs today. Some of the hollows are already cut off by water, so those are out, but several aren't flooded yet. We'll try to deliver one meal where it's possible, and we'll do it in convoys of two. The ERV will haul the food, and the other driver will ride 'shotgun,' like in the Wild West movies. While two of you deliver food, the other vehicle can follow to provide for emergencies. That way, you'll have help if you need it. I don't want any of you stranded in high water."

From radio reports, the road into Newberry Hollow wasn't yet blocked, so Amelia and Chase loaded the heavy insulated containers as soon as the food was prepared. There had been no letup in the rainfall by the time they started out. It was comforting to know that Rick followed them in his SUV.

When they came to a fork where two different streams converged, Chase stopped for a conference with Rick. The right tributary led to Newberry Hollow. Turbulent, muddy water poured down the left fork of the stream. Water was several inches below the floor of the bridge that spanned the stream where the two forks converged.

"That happens sometimes," Rick explained. "There might be a cloudburst in one hollow, but the mountains keep it from raining only a few miles away.''

Rick and Chase assessed the strength of the bridge, and after monitoring the rise of the water for fifteen minutes, Rick said, ''The rain seems to be letting up now, and the creek may not get over the bridge at all. Even if it does, you'll probably have enough time to deliver the food. The water may have reached its crest now, but I don't know. It's up to you.''

Knowing that people in the hollow needed the food, Chase decided to go on.

''I'll wait on this side of the creek,'' Rick said. ''No use stressing the bridge with my van as well as the ERV. That way, I'll be here if you have trouble coming back. Is this the only place you have to cross the creek?''

Chase nodded, and turned to Amelia. ''You stay here, too.''

''No!'' she said emphatically. ''Chase, I'd be miserable wondering what was happening. You go, I go.''

He'd seen the steely determination in her eyes often enough to know that he'd waste time arguing with her. He waved to Rick and held the door open for Amelia. With some apprehension, he drove the vehicle across the bridge, hoping that the water wouldn't rise much until they returned. Strangely enough, this new storm hadn't flooded any of the houses on the branch of the creek where Josh and Mandy lived.

"We had some rain, but nothing like we had before," Josh reported, after Mandy and he greeted them in their usual openhearted manner. "We watched the rain all night, and from the distant thunder we heard, I think there was a cloudburst on yon side of the mountain. I appreciate you coming, but get out of here right away."

But Chase wouldn't leave until he'd given food to all the families living in the hollow. More than an hour elapsed before they returned to where Rick waited.

When they neared the bridge, Amelia gasped, and she placed her hand on Chase's arm. Water was lapping at the concrete floor of the bridge, and Rick was pacing back and forth along the creek bank. He shouted, "We're not supposed to drive through water, but there's none on the bridge yet. Hurry."

Chapter Twelve

Unbuckling his seat belt, Chase said, "Get out, Amelia, and walk across."

"But, Chase..." she started to protest.

"I said get out and walk across. Now!"

Amelia glanced at him momentarily. His face was ashen, and the tone in his voice was like a whiplash. He'd never used that tone of voice to her before. Amelia opened the door and obeyed.

The sooner she was on safe ground, the sooner Chase could bring across the ERV. She wanted to run, but the concrete floor was muddy. She didn't dare slip. When she was across, Rick motioned to Chase. He stood in the middle of the roadway, his feet touching the bridge, so Chase could use him as a guide.

Amelia didn't want to watch Chase drive over that

fast-flowing, muddy stream, and she closed her eyes, but they popped open of their own accord. She couldn't stop looking— she had to know what was happening. She knew Chase had made her walk because he was apprehensive of the bridge. If he had any trouble, he wanted her safe. Why was he afraid? It wasn't a very wide creek, and the bridge looked stable. Surely he'd make it all right

She dropped to her knees, praying, *"God, give him safety. He's precious to me. I love him. I love him,"* she said over and over, not realizing her heart was verbalizing the words.

Chase drove calmly and efficiently as he steered toward Rick's solid form. When he was within a few feet of the approach, she expelled a pent-up breath.

"He's going to make it," she said to Rick.

But when the ERV was within a foot of the end of the bridge, she heard a crack as loud as cannon fire. Someone was screaming, and Amelia realized it was her own voice. She ran toward the creek as the bridge slowly folded and toppled the ERV into the water.

"God, have mercy," Rick Smith shouted, and he ran toward the wreckage. Her knees shook so much, Amelia fell to the ground and crawled on hands and knees to the water's edge.

The driver's side of the ERV was underwater, but she could see the top of Chase's head. The passen ger's side of the vehicle, where he'd been thrown, perched high and dry against the bank.

"What can we do?" she whispered to Rick.

His trembling voice and panic-stricken expression weren't encouraging. "The ERV is tight and will keep the water out for a while, but we don't have much time. I've been watching the creek while you were away, and it's risen almost a foot in an hour."

"We've got to get him out."

"If he's penned in, or injured, I don't know how we can."

"We can't stand here and watch him drown. Do something! Chase!" she screamed. "Chase!"

As if the sound of her voice reached him, Chase stirred and opened his eyes.

"Can you move?" Rick shouted.

"He'd unbuckled his seat belt before I got out."

They watched as Chase squirmed round in the seat and pulled himself upward. Motioning, Rick shouted, "Climb to the passenger's door. If you can't open the window, I'll break it. Watch him, Amelia," Rick said as he hurried toward his van. "Good thing I loaded a sledgehammer in my vehicle."

Water swirled around the door of the ERV where it leaned against the muddy bank. It seemed impossible that the door would open until a wrecker pulled the car free. A sinking feeling in her stomach, Amelia knew this was no time to panic. Chase pushed on the button to open the window, but it wouldn't budge. He shook his head. Rick rushed to the bank with a sledgehammer and walked close to the ERV with water lapping at his boots.

"Cover your head," he shouted. Chase nodded his understanding and pulled his jacket over his head.

Rick crushed the window with one blow, and continued chopping away at the glass until the opening was relatively free of glass. Dropping the sledgehammer, he extended his hand to Chase and pulled him out of the vehicle, just as the ground underneath gave way and the ERV rolled over and submerged in the water.

Chase collapsed on the ground, gasping for breath, but his only injury seemed to be cuts on his hands from the flying glass. Amelia crawled to Chase and put her arms around him. She covered his face with kisses, while tears ran from her eyes and moistened his face.

"I've never been so frightened in my life," she whispered.

With a weak grin, he said, "I was a little scared, too."

Rick had turned his SUV while they'd been delivering food, and he said, "We need to get out of here. This whole road may be covered before long. But first, let's thank God for His mercy."

"Yes, please," Chase murmured.

Amelia held tightly to Chase's hand as Rick gave glory to God for saving Chase's life. He helped Chase to his feet, saying, "I'm sorry, Chase. I shouldn't have allowed you to drive across, but I thought the water had crested. I'll probably get chewed out good and proper by headquarters for losing that ERV, but I had to make a split-second decision."

Amelia got in the back seat so Chase could have the front seat as they went back to town. Nervous reaction had set in. She shook until her teeth chattered, and she couldn't control her sobs. What if she'd had to stand helplessly and watch Chase drown?

Chase turned and put one of his injured hands on her trembling knee. "It's all right, Melly, don't cry. Everything turned out all right."

Amelia couldn't stop crying. She'd shed more tears in the past two weeks than she had in the fifteen years she'd been separated from Chase.

When they came to the motel, Rick stopped. "As soon as I report the loss of the ERV to headquarters, I'm going to take Chase to the hospital. His cuts have to be treated, and I want a doctor to examine him. Amelia, you'd better take the rest of the day off."

Amelia didn't argue. She handed Rick the keys to her car. "Take these to Vicky, please, so she'll have a way to get back to the motel tonight. That way, the car will be here when I need it in the morning. Thanks for being there, Rick. I couldn't have managed if we'd been alone today."

"It wasn't just happenstance that caused me to go with you," he said. "God knew you'd need help today."

Without looking at Chase, she stepped out of the vehicle and made her way on wobbly knees to the motel. In her concern for Chase, she'd made a spectacle of herself. What did Rick think of her actions? What conclusions had Chase drawn? She wasn't sure what she'd said, but there wasn't any doubt that she'd revealed not only to the others, but to herself, that she still loved Chase.

Removing her muddy jeans and shoes, she collapsed on the bed. Why couldn't she stop shaking? She took a blanket from the closet and wrapped it around herself and eventually dozed off into a semi-conscious state. A knock on the door awakened her.

She shrugged quickly into a robe and went to the door, and through the peephole saw that Chase was outside. She opened the door. His hands had several small bandages.

"Is it all right if I come in?"

"Of course." As she closed the door behind him, she asked, "How are you?"

"The cuts were minor, but the doctor cleaned the wounds and medicated them. I did have a bump on the back of my head, and I suppose that's why I was unconscious for a minute or two. She told me to take it easy the rest of the day.''

Amelia sat on her bed and propped pillows behind her back. Motioning to Vicky's bed, she said, ''Sit, or lie down, whichever you need the most. I have no energy at all, and your day was worse than mine.''

He sat wearily on the bed, removed his shoes, lay down on his side, facing her. ''I probably shouldn't stay here, but I don't want to be alone right now.''

''That's understandable. You've been through a terrible ordeal.''

''You and Rick probably experienced the most trauma. I exerted all of my energy trying to get out of the ERV, and I didn't have any time to think about what could happen. But I'm getting tired now.''

''Vicky won't mind if you nap on her bed.''

''If it's okay with you, I'll do that. Reaction is setting in now, when I realize what might have happened.''

''I still need to rest, too, and I'd like you to stay. But let's not talk about the accident. I want to get it off my mind.''

She closed her eyes, wondering if they should stay in the same room, because there was a limit to how much temptation they could endure. The beds were only separated by a few feet. Were they still married in the sight of God, regardless of the divorce decree? Amelia wouldn't let her thoughts go any further.

By his even breathing, she knew when Chase slept, and she turned on her side so she could watch him. What did the future hold for them? She knew now that she was ready to be Chase's wife again, but there were so many things to consider, not least of which that they both had jobs in widely separated cities. One of them would have to relocate.

Trying to be quiet so she wouldn't wake Chase, Amelia sat up in bed and piled the pillows behind her again. She hadn't yet been able to stop her inner trembling—she could still see Chase lying unconscious in the vehicle with that turbulent stream flowing around him. She picked up her Bible from the bedside table and prayed for God to guide her to a Scripture that would calm her inner turmoil. Holding the Bible in her hand, eyes closed, she prayed silently. *God, thank You for saving his life. Give me calmness of spirit. Now that the ordeal is over, I should just be thankful for his deliverance, but I can't stop thinking what might have happened. Forgive me for my lack of faith.*

When Amelia wanted to praise God, she always turned to the Psalms, and when she was troubled, she found comfort and strength there. Today, she needed to praise God and receive comfort, too. As she looked at the last few verses of the ninety-first

Psalm, she whispered the words of the psalmist that seemed applicable to Chase's ordeal.

"'Because he loves me,'" says the Lord, "'I will rescue him; I will protect him, for he acknowledges my name. He will call upon me, and I will answer him; I will be with him in trouble, I will deliver him and honor him. With long life will I satisfy him and show him my salvation.'"

She took those words as God's promise that Chase would have a long life in which to serve God. Would she stand by his side as Chase fulfilled God's purpose for his life?

Chase groaned, opened his eyes and turned on his back. Amelia swung her feet to the floor and sat on the side on the bed.

"How do you feel?" she asked softly.

"Lousy," he said. "My head hurts."

"I have some aspirin. Do you want to take some?"

He took a bottle from his pocket. "The doctor gave me some pain medicine. I'll go to my room, take some of these and I'll probably go to sleep again."

He yawned and sat up stiffly. "Rick gave orders that we're to take tomorrow off. He thinks the local roads will be closed, so we won't have much work to do anyway. We can drive a few miles north and get away from the flooded areas."

"How can we go anyplace if the roads are closed?"

"We'll see what roads are open when tomorrow comes, if you want to get away for a few hours."

"Yes, I want to go with you. When I go back to Philadelphia, I don't know when I'll see you again." The way she felt now, she didn't want Chase out of her sight.

He sat beside her on the bed. "We need a day to ourselves to find out where we go from here. An experience like we had this morning puts a new perspective on the priorities in life."

She wouldn't meet his gaze, but she said, "I know. I'm still shaking inside. I don't know if I'll ever be able to ride in an ERV again."

He put his arm around her, wondering if it was wise. They were both vulnerable now, and it would be easy to act without thinking. He squeezed her shoulders and stood, pulling her up with him.

"We both need to rest. Let's have dinner together tonight."

She turned toward Chase and put her arms around him and leaned her head against his shoulder. She knew it was right for him to go to his room, but she couldn't stop thinking that, by the space of a few minutes, Chase would have been in the ERV when it toppled into the creek. Would she ever want to be separated from him again?

"I don't know what the future holds for us," she

whispered, "but if I'd lost you today, life wouldn't have had much meaning for me. I believe I've just been existing the years we've been separated, not living. Let's pray about what we should do from now on. I want God's perfect will to be done in my life, but I hope His will includes you."

"Do you know what I thought when it seemed as if I couldn't be saved?" he said in a husky voice. "I thought I'd waited too long to tell you how much you mean to me. Melly," he murmured, his words as intimate as a caress, "I love you. I always have."

A smile of tenderness hovered around his mouth. She made no attempt to evade his lips, but raised her face eagerly to his. He kissed her again and again. The caresses were so sweet, so all-consuming, that their clinging lips said what they couldn't verbally express. The bitterness of the past fled away.

Chase eased her from him gently. "I'll telephone in a few hours."

Amelia moved out of his arms without protest. When the door closed behind him, she lay on the bed and tried to clear her mind to get some sleep. She needed to make decisions, but her thoughts were too chaotic and her emotions too raw for serious contemplation. A month ago, her life was all mapped out—she was resigned to move from middle age into the future alone, believing that all would be well. How wrong she'd been!

While she waited for Chase to call, she dressed

and sat staring out the window. The residential section of Williamson was located on the mountainside—the houses, built a third of the way up the hill, were so close together there didn't seem to be more than ten feet between any dwelling. Most of the frame houses appeared to have been built in the early part of the twentieth century, although a few brick structures had been built more recently.

The inn was separated from the mountain by several railroad tracks that had been opened for train traffic to resume. Two trains, pulling loaded coal cars, passed while she waited for Chase. The building vibrated from the movement of the train, and Amelia wondered how they would be able to sleep if the trains ran throughout the night. But coal mining was the lifeline of this community, so many trains meant a good economy.

Chase looked more rested when he came to the door.

"Ready?" he asked.

"Yes. How are you feeling?" she said as she closed the door behind her.

"All right."

"How could you sleep with the trains going by?"

As they walked down the hall to the elevator, he said, "I didn't hear any trains."

They made a quick stop at the church parking lot so Amelia could get a sweater from her car. The restaurant had been chilly when she'd been there before.

"We're a little early for the main dinner crowd," Chase said as the hostess seated them in the dining room.

"It's a treat to be able to eat in a restaurant occasionally," Amelia said. "The food we've been having is good, but it's nice to sit down and be served, instead of serving ourselves."

When the waiter took their order, he asked, "One check or two?"

"Two," Amelia said.

"One," Chase said simultaneously.

The waiter laughed pleasantly. "I'll bring two checks and you can battle it out between you."

For the main entrée, Chase ordered rib-eye steak and Amelia asked for glazed pork chops. As soon as the waiter left them, Chase turned steely gray eyes on Amelia.

His brows drawn together in an angry frown, Chase said sternly, "I asked you to have dinner with me. I'm paying the bill."

Shrinking away from him in a feigned attitude of terror, Amelia said faintly, "Yes, *sir!*"

Chase grinned sheepishly. "I guess I don't have the right to order you around. But I feel like we're out on a date, and I should pick up the tab like I used to."

Changing the subject, Amelia motioned to the window and said, "That's a nice view, isn't it?"

Apparently, she wasn't ready to deal with their

future, so while they waited for salads and beverages, he listened as Amelia talked about their surroundings. They were seated at a corner table, where they had a good view of the earthen floodwall dike. Although it served a utilitarian purpose, the landscaped trees and shrubbery made it look like a park. Above the concrete floodwall, they could see the mountains across the Tug Fork River in Kentucky.

The dining room itself had a touch of the past mingled with the modern. The twelve-electric-candle brass chandelier bathed the room with a muted light. Brass wall sconces held three candles each. Photos of Williamson's past were on the walls, along with an extensive plate collection.

As they were leaving the restaurant, the cashier asked, "Have you strolled along the floodwall walkway? It's a nice place for an evening walk. You can access the area in several places by steps like the ones outside our building."

"Shall we walk?" Chase asked when they went outside.

"Yes. Some exercise might help me rest tonight. I'm afraid to go to sleep, fearful I'll dream about what happened today."

Chase took her hand as they walked toward the dike.

"Honey, you'll have to forget about it. I'm all right. For some reason, God saved my life today.

Just be thankful I escaped, and don't worry about what could have happened.''

''I know that's what I should do, but that scene is seared on my mind. I'll never forget it.''

With hands interlocked, they walked slowly along the broad walk built along the concrete barrier. In a few places, they could see the floodwaters tumbling toward the Ohio River, but for the most part, they enjoyed the trees planted along the dike. A robin entertained them with his vibrato song as they walked by the pine tree where he perched on the top branch.

Darkness approached quickly in the deep mountain valley as soon as the sun sank from sight. Many of the Red Cross volunteers returning from their day's work were gathering in the motel when she and Chase returned. They encountered Vicky, who rode up in the elevator with them, and Amelia said goodbye to Chase, whose room was on the top floor.

His lingering glance, studying her with full intensity as the elevator door closed between them, left Amelia with conflicting emotions. She felt a sudden sadness that she would be deprived of his company until morning.

Chapter Thirteen

The next morning, Chase and Amelia started out after breakfast. A light mist covered the windshield of his truck as Chase drove through the floodwall gate and turned north on the highway.

"If it continues to rain, we won't be able to do much sightseeing," Chase said, "but we can be together." Slanting a glance in her direction, he said, "It's almost like we're starting on another honeymoon."

"Now, Chase, don't presume. I'm not sure yet. Twenty years ago, our lives weren't molded as they are now. We didn't know enough to consider the consequences then. Now we do. There are others to consider besides ourselves. My parents will be pleased. They've always liked you, and if you're responsible for me, they won't feel obligated. Your parents won't like it, though."

''My parents know I haven't been happy with my life. Maybe they suspect that losing you did that to me. I think they'll be different—we've all had time to change. But I won't pressure you today.''

''Where are we going?''

''To Heritage Farm, a two-hour drive from Williamson. Rick recommended it and thought we'd be able to reach the site. There are lots of interesting attractions in the southern counties of the state, but with the flood damage, many of those places are difficult to reach.''

They had to take a few detours, because the main highway was flooded in several places, but the drive was a pleasant one. The curvy road commanded much of Chase's attention and necessitated a moderate speed. Since Chase had to keep his eyes on the road, Amelia commented frequently on the countryside. Except for a few pasture fields where cattle grazed, and many small gardens, they saw very little level ground. Expensive homes had been built at the base of the high, tree-covered mountains dominated by steep rock cliffs. Villages were located near the road, which followed various rivers and creeks before they reached their destination.

Heritage Farm Museum and Village, organized to preserve Appalachian heritage, provided a step back in time. The exhibits were eye-opening to both Chase and Amelia who knew very little of Appalachian culture. They signed up for a two-hour tour.

While they waited for the tour to start, they looked at an introductory brochure.

"'This site depicts life in Appalachia from the 1850s through the 1950s,'" Chase read aloud.

The two hours passed quickly as they visited several restored log cabins furnished with rural displays—a transportation exhibit, farm implements, a blacksmith shop, antique cars and engines, spinning and weaving exhibits.

After the tour ended, Amelia and Chase returned to the log beam church, known as a meeting house in pioneer days. They sat, shoulders touching, on an ornate church pew and listened to music from a player piano.

Amelia didn't recognize the name of the song, and she said, "Do you know that song?"

"I can't remember the title, but it has something to do with peace. As the music played, I've remembered a few of the lyrics. One verse testifies to the security we have as Christians—'And I'm kept from all danger by night and by day.' Sitting here, I feel the security and peace that God gives us."

Amelia reached into her purse and pulled out a small New Testament. She turned to the book of Philippians.

"I'm ashamed of my fears for the last twenty-four hours, and I'm resting in God's peace now. I love this verse," she said, reading aloud from the Testament, "'And the peace of God, which transcends all understanding, will guard your hearts and your minds in Christ Jesus.'''

"With that promise, we don't have to be frustrated by what has happened or what the future holds." His voice softened, and he regarded her with a tender gaze. "Let's pray together before we leave."

Amelia slipped to her knees on the hard, wooden floor and, holding her hand, Chase knelt beside her.

"Lord Jesus," he said, "we thank You for the peace that we can claim because of what You did for us at Calvary. And today, we need a double portion of Your peace to erase yesterday's near-tragedy from our memory. If it had been my time to die, I would have been in heaven today, and there wouldn't have been regrets. But You didn't take me, so You must have a reason for me to continue my earthly life. Amelia and I stand at the crossroads. We've made mistakes, and we pray for guidance and wisdom to make the future better than the past. Amen."

Amelia lifted her head and turned misty brown eyes toward him. "I believe God will answer that prayer," she said.

"Yes, He will, but we may have to be patient a little longer until we know where He's leading. I know what *I* want, but only if it's best for both of us."

When they left Heritage Village, Amelia said, "I

noticed dozens of yard sales when we were driving this morning. One of them had books advertised for sale. Let's stop there on our return to Williamson. Maybe we can find books for the flood victims.'' She looked at him with a no-nonsense gleam in her eye. ''And I'm paying for them!''

''Yes, *ma'am*,'' he said in mock humility.

Amelia knew they'd struck pay dirt when they stopped at that sale and she saw the card table filled with children's books. A nearby table held numerous paperbacks.

''Will you go through the children's books and choose only the ones in good condition?'' she asked. ''I'll check these novels to see which ones look the most interesting. We'll need books to please the reading tastes of both men and women.''

She chose enough paperbacks to fill two grocery bags, and Chase had more than fifty books in his box. When the owner learned why they wanted the books, she absolutely refused to take any money.

''Take them, and welcome,'' she insisted. ''I've been wondering what I can do to help the flood victims. I want to donate the books.''

''That's good of you,'' Amelia said, thanking the woman. She appreciated the woman's generosity, but after observing the small mobile home, and the several children in the family, she pressed a twenty-dollar bill into the woman's hand. ''Take your children out for hamburgers and fries tonight, on me.''

''Thank you,'' the woman said.

''Had a good day?'' Chase asked as they neared the disaster area.

''Very good. I'm eager and ready to get back to work. Did you have a good time?''

''Yes, except for one thing.''

When she turned quizzical eyes toward him, he said, ''I haven't kissed you all day.''

''Well, whose fault is that?''

They were in an isolated area, and as soon as Chase found a berm wide enough for him to park the truck, he pulled off the highway. Chase gathered Amelia into his arms and held her snugly before his lips captured hers in a tender kiss as light and invigorating as the spring breeze that wafted the scent of plum blossoms through the windows.

Amelia and Chase reported to the center the next morning, ready to resume their duties. Since the Red Cross teams were already in the area and well organized, they could provide immediate help to the second round of flood victims. The damage wasn't as widespread as the previous flood had been. Some areas that had flooded a month earlier had no water, and most of the damage came from creeks that were fed by cloudbursts on the mountains.

Rick assigned them to a subdivision of new homes, where several feet of water had rushed through houses in a fast-moving deluge. As they approached with the food, people stood in forlorn groups looking helplessly at their homes, as if they couldn't believe the damage. Unlike many of the moderate dwellings that had been ruined in the earlier flood, these homes were expensive buildings of brick and stone. Their sturdy structure and foundations had resisted the onslaught, but the force of the water had broken windows and forced doors open and flooded the interiors. Wearing shorts and high rubber boots, several families swept the muddy water out of their homes. Piles of ruined furniture were stacked outside the homes.

"Déjà vu," Chase said.

"I was thinking the same thing," Amelia answered. "This seems like a nightmare of what we encountered two weeks ago. Same problem, different hollow."

"We had no time to save anything," one man told Chase. "Several inches of rain fell in a couple of hours. I've lived around these parts for a long time, and I know how fast the creek can rise when there's a downpour on the mountains. I knew we had to go to higher ground. One good thing, it came in daylight, and we had time to reach safety, even if we couldn't save our houses. It almost tore the heart right out of my chest when I had to watch my home getting destroyed."

"How many houses have been affected in this area?" Chase asked.

"A dozen or so," the man answered. "This used to be a mining town, and the developer bought the land from the mine owners, tore down the old company houses and built new ones."

The man and his wife were grateful for the hot food Chase and Amelia served them.

"You'll find the other houses farther up the hollow. Far as I know, the bridges are all right."

Amelia and Chase exchanged glances, but accepted the man's thanks and drove away.

"We'll carry the food rather than to risk any more bridges," Chase said. "The insurance company has totaled the ERV. I feel responsible to a certain extent, but Rick said not to worry about it."

"You know how my parents like to fling their money around, so last night I wrote them a letter, explaining what had happened to us. I hinted subtly that they might want to contribute money to purchase a new ERV for this area."

"Do you think they'll do it?"

"Sure. It will give them an opportunity to have their pictures in the papers."

"You shouldn't be so sarcastic about your parents."

"I know, and I'm ashamed of myself when I am, but after all these years, I don't have any delusions about what prompts their charitable contributions."

"Did you mention that I was driving the ERV?"

"Yes, I did. That will influence their decision. As far as I know, they've never contributed much to the American Red Cross, and they should. Now that I've seen firsthand how the organization meets the needs of disaster victims, I'm going to help with fund-raising."

Everywhere they stopped to deliver meals they encountered the same situation. Each house had been flooded, and the fast-moving water had left behind mud and debris in the buildings and yards. Near the head of the hollow, a two-story brick house had been built close to the creek and seemed to have suffered more destruction than the others farther downstream.

At this home, a woman came to the door with a push broom in her hand. Amelia recognized her at once, because this woman's face had seared her memory fifteen years ago. She darted a quick look toward Chase, but his view of the woman was obscured by the ERV.

The woman's jeans were rolled to her knees, she wore plastic boots and a scarf was tied around her hair. Rosemary had changed a lot, but the hard, cynical expression in her eyes had survived the years.

"Well, well," the woman said. "Fancy meeting you at this time and place!"

Chase was busy opening the rear panel of the ERV, but at her words he turned quickly.

"Rosemary!" he said, and the horror on his face convinced Amelia that he wasn't happy to see his former girlfriend. Would his reaction have been different if Amelia hadn't been with him? Immediately, the affection she'd felt for Chase the past few days disappeared, and her old doubts and disappointments surfaced. Was this woman destined to spoil things between Chase and her again?

The years apparently hadn't been kind to Rosemary. She'd gained weight, maybe as much as twenty or thirty pounds, but she was tall enough that the weight hadn't hurt her appearance. Her hair was no longer brown, but a honey-blond color, styled in a fashionable short cut that complemented her dark blue eyes set in an oval face. Her eyes were hard and filled with bitterness, a normal expression under the circumstances. Amelia wondered if Rosemary wasn't bitter over past mistakes, because there was a cynical twist to her mouth, and the passage of time had carved merciless lines on her face.

"Sorry I can't ask you in for a cup of coffee," Rosemary said derisively. "My coffeemaker is piled in the middle of the kitchen floor with a lot of other debris."

A girl, who appeared to be about ten years old, came to the door. "Who is it, Mother?" she said. The girl held a young child by the hand.

"People from the Red Cross," Rosemary said.

"How many trays of food do you need?" Amelia

forced herself to say as she had to the other people they'd served that morning.

"There are five of us," Rosemary said. "My husband and son are working in the basement, seeing if there's anything to salvage."

After first recognizing Rosemary, Chase hadn't said anything, but he refused to meet Amelia's eyes as they carried the food to a table on the patio. The concrete patio pad had been hosed off, and the table cleaned, so it was a decent place for them to eat.

"We had this table chained down, or we'd have lost it," Rosemary said as she lifted her younger daughter to one of the benches. After her children, whom she introduced as Ashley and Jordan, started eating, Rosemary came to the ERV where Amelia and Chase worked in silence.

"There are things in my past that I haven't told my husband," she said quietly. "I'd appreciate it if you don't say anything."

"Sure, Rosemary," Chase said. "I'm pleased to know that you're happily married."

As she took the container of juice that Amelia handed her, Rosemary said, "I thought you two got a divorce."

"We did," Amelia said, determined not to let Rosemary realize how this meeting had riveted a new pain in her heart. She could make allowances for the woman today, after seeing what her loss had been.

"And you're back together?"

"Not exactly," Chase said. "We met again when both of us came to work in the Red Cross relief effort."

Rosemary seemed to find that amusing, for she laughed. Surveying Amelia's unkempt clothing, she said, "You've come down a notch or two in life."

"Amelia has been working in disaster relief for two weeks." Chase jumped to her defense. "You can't expect her to look like she did in college."

"Still quick to take her side, I see."

"When did you move to this area?" Chase asked, searching frantically for a less prickly subject. "The last I heard, you were in California."

Rosemary shrugged her shoulders. "I went to the Long Beach area and married a sailor, thinking marriage to him would give me a chance to see the world. Five years and three kids later, he decided he didn't want his children to be shifted around as navy kids, so he left the service. He'd been raised in this area, and he wanted to come back home. We've lived here for three years."

Rosemary looked around bitterly. "I was just becoming adjusted to living in the boondocks, and now we've lost everything."

"You still have three children," Amelia said. "I wouldn't consider that losing everything."

"Spoken like a woman who doesn't have any," Rosemary said. "Or at least I'm assuming that you don't have any children—you're as thin as you were when you stole Chase away from me.''

Amelia wondered if Rosemary knew that her words were turning a knife in an old wound. But how could she? Until she'd unburdened herself to Chase a few days ago, Amelia had never shared with anyone her deep pain because she couldn't have children. She turned away from the bitterness in the woman's words and in her eyes. At least one thing hadn't changed—Rosemary still hadn't lost her desire for Chase. And would Chase be tempted again?

''Chase, let's go,'' Amelia said. ''We have more deliveries to make.'' To Rosemary, she said, ''Are there any messages you want us to deliver? Any phone calls to make?''

''Not right now,'' she said. ''My husband moved our car to higher ground and saved it from the flood, so we can drive out of the hollow. Don't bring us any more food, either. We don't need charity.''

They traveled out of the hollow in silence. Rosemary had never been a safe subject between them. At last Chase said, ''I'm sorry we ran into her.''

''And just when I'd decided things were going well for us,'' Amelia agreed. ''I'd had enough without being reminded of Rosemary and the darkest period of my life. I've been considering whether to go home or stay on for a while, but I know now that it's time for me to leave this area.''

''So you're running away.''

"I guess that's it. Sometimes it's easier to run than stay and fight. I need a break."

"A break from me?"

"Maybe. We made two mistakes, Chase. I don't want to make another one."

"Two mistakes?"

"I was going to say our marriage and a hasty divorce, but I'm not sure our marriage was a mistake. A second one might be."

"How could it be? I love you and I think you still love me. If nothing else came out of my near-drowning experience, it taught me that I still want you, want to be married to you. And the wretched look on your face when you thought I might die convinces me that you still care for me, too."

"I'd have felt wretched to have seen a complete stranger perish that way, so that doesn't prove your point."

"Look me straight in the eye and tell me you don't love me."

She laughed slightly. "You're driving, and this road is treacherous. Keep your eyes on the road."

"Don't sidestep the issue," Chase said, and Amelia knew he was angry. But why was he angry? Had seeing Rosemary again revived old feelings? Was he diverting the anger he felt for himself toward Amelia?

Biting her lip to stop its trembling, Amelia said,

with a sob in her voice, "I'm embarrassed to admit to the world that we were foolish to get a divorce. We've both made separate lives of our own. Maybe that's the way it's supposed to be."

Chapter Fourteen

They traveled several miles in silence, and when they came to Newberry Hollow, Chase slowed down.

"Want to check on Josh and Mandy?"

"Yes. I always feel better when I see them."

Josh and Mandy had heard them coming, and they stood on the porch waving a welcome when Chase stopped the ERV in front of their house. First, Amelia and Chase were invited to take a tour of their refurbished home. One wall of the living room was decorated with photographs of their children and grandchildren. Josh took down one picture from the wall.

"Three boys and three girls," Josh said. The picture, taken on the occasion of the Newberrys' fiftieth wedding anniversary, was one Chase and Amelia had seen on their last visit. "I'm proud of all my kids," he said.

"You have a right to be," Amelia said sincerely, noting again the stalwart sons who resembled their father. Two of the girls were fair like their mother, but Emily had a pert little face and seemed to have a personality different from the others. Not that Amelia had ever aspired to have such a large family, but seeing the Newberrys' offspring made her realize again how little she had to show for her forty-three years. Amelia tried to brighten her features when she sensed Mandy's concerned gaze in her direction.

When Josh and Chase went to the barn to see a new calf, Mandy said, "I don't like to meddle in your business, Amelia, but you're sad, and I'd like to help. What's bothering you?"

Mandy had always shown Amelia the sympathetic concern she'd longed for from her mother, but she'd carried the burden of her failed marriage for so long that it was hard to talk about it.

When Amelia hesitated, Mandy said, "Your secret is safe with me. I've got so many secrets stored up in my heart that I'm like a walking encyclopedia."

"Do you remember the time Josh asked if Chase and I had been married?"

"Yes, I recollect how fussed up you were about the question."

"Chase said that both of us had been married and divorced. The truth of the matter is, we were married to each other for five years."

"You don't say!" Mandy said, surprise spreading across her wrinkled face. "I knew there was something between you, but I didn't suspect that."

"We hadn't seen each other for fifteen years until we came to help in the flood recovery."

Briefly, Amelia explained about their marriage, subsequent divorce and the reason for it. "It was a terrible emotional surprise when chance brought us together again."

"Chance didn't have nothing to do with it," Mandy said bluntly. "It was the hand of God workin' in your lives. When God joined you together, He meant for you to stay that way."

"I was beginning to think that, too, but today we accidentally encountered Rosemary, the woman Chase was involved with. All the old doubts came back again."

"Amelia, you haven't asked for advice, but take it from an old woman who's seen about every problem possible—you've got to come to grips with that situation and let it go. Let it go, Amelia. You'll be miserable until you do."

"You may be right. I'm miserable enough now."

Hearing footsteps on the porch, Amelia was saved from further advice when Chase and Josh entered the room. Chase looked quickly from Mandy to

Amelia as if he sensed the tension in the room.
Amelia stood quickly to avoid any questions, and
they soon took their leave of the Newberrys.

The return drive to Williamson was made almost
in silence, with only a few perfunctory remarks.
When Rick hustled out of headquarters when they
drove in, Chase said, "Now what? I almost dread
to return from a day's work—seems there's always
some new crisis."

Chase lowered the window when Rick reached
them.

"We had a message, relayed through the state police, that you should call the bank where you're em-
ployed. The telephone company has set up a rack of
phones behind the church now, so you can call from
here."

"Will you wait until I see what this is about?"
Chase asked Amelia.

"Yes. I'll see if I can beg some coffee from the
cook tent." As Chase headed toward the phones, she
stepped wearily out of the ERV, and Rick said,
"Had a rough day?"

"Yes, but not as bad as the people who've had
another flood. Will it ever stop raining?"

"For what it's worth, the forecast says the storms
are over. But I figure this new deluge had added
another month or two to our work here."

Amelia asked for two containers of coffee, and
she sat alone and sipped the hot brew slowly. She

kept thinking of Mandy's words—"When God joined you together, He meant for you to stay that way."

Was it time for her and Chase to put the past behind them, forget the objections of their respective families and find what happiness they could? They'd reached the mellow years, but they should still have quite a bit of time ahead of them. They could never redeem the lost years, but why not take advantage of the future? Should she let her doubts separate them again?

Chase slid to the bench beside her, and she handed a container of coffee to him.

"Bad news?" she asked.

"Yes and no. I have to return to Ohio right away—that's the bad news. But the good news is that a big loan deal that I've been negotiating has gone through. I have to be at work tomorrow to take care of the final details."

"Will you come back?"

"I don't think so. I either have to stay at my job or quit. I've used all of my vacation time, and I can't ask the bank for more leave." He finished the coffee and took their containers to the waste bin. "I've already told Rick I'm leaving. I'm going to the motel to pack. Will you come with me?"

She didn't answer, but stood and walked by his side to his truck.

"I'll stay at the motel. I gave Vicky the extra key to my car—she'll bring it when she finishes work."

"You're intending to return to Philadelphia next week?"

"Yes."

"Will you let me come see you there? I can come by plane on a weekend when I'm not working."

"Yes. I don't want you to go out of my life again."

"I'll give you my business and home phone numbers, so you can contact me when you're back in Philadelphia. Actually, I think we'll be able to look at the future better when we're in another setting. Our emotions have been so involved with the tragedy of these people that it's difficult to zero in on our own problems."

While he packed, Amelia went to her room, washed her face and combed her hair. She even put on makeup, something she hadn't done for days. If she was going to be separated from Chase, she didn't want him to remember her as a bedraggled shrew. While she was working to help everyone, her appearance hadn't mattered, but she hurried to put on a clean blouse and pants so Chase would have at least one pleasant memory of her.

Fifteen minutes later when he knocked on the door, she took a glance at herself in the mirror. She wasn't displeased.

Chase stepped inside and set his luggage on the

floor. He'd also changed his clothes, and he looked more like the man she'd married. He reached for her, and she went willingly into his arms, her head resting on his shoulder.

"I hate to leave you," he whispered into her hair. "There's so much danger down here. Will you be careful?"

She nodded.

"You can call now from the portable phone booths at the Red Cross headquarters. I'll be at work tomorrow, and if you can't call then, call my home over the weekend."

He leaned away from her and searched her eyes intently.

"I'd like to have you tell me something I haven't heard for a long time. Don't say it to make me feel good—only if you really mean it."

She knew what he meant. Momentarily, Rosemary's face flashed into her mind. She took a deep breath, knowing this was a turning point for them. "Yes, I love you, but I'm not promising anything."

He squeezed her until she gasped for breath.

"Then we'll be able to work things out between us. I believe love will conquer any problem. Let's stop dwelling on the past. We have a future, Amelia. I want to share it with you."

He kissed her then, and they shared a blissful moment, too deep for words. She clung to him, joying in the strength of his embrace, savoring the sure knowledge that he returned her love. Before he released her, Chase kissed the tip of her nose.

"Be careful, Melly," he said. "I can't live without you."

Amelia scurried to the window so she could watch him drive from the parking lot. She experienced an unbearable sense of loss to be separated from him. Her thoughts of his indiscretion had to be put aside.

The next morning, when Vicky and Amelia reported for duty, Rick hesitantly asked Amelia if she would drive an ERV and make a few deliveries.

"I know you've had some pretty unpleasant experiences driving in the area," he said, "and I wouldn't ask you except I'm shorthanded."

"I don't know how much help I'll be," Vicky said, "but I'll go with her, if it's okay with you, Rick."

Vicky's distress for the past few days had convinced Amelia that her feelings for Allen Chambers were deeper than mere infatuation, and that she was really hurting because he didn't return her love. Although she was frightened to drive the ERV, she agreed to make the run for Vicky's sake, as much as the flood victims who needed help.

"I want you to go into the housing area where you and Chase were yesterday."

Of all the flood relief areas, this was the one place Amelia didn't want to go, but she couldn't refuse without giving a reason, which she wouldn't do. She had to come to the point where she could look at Rosemary and acknowledge, "This woman had an affair with my husband, but it's over now, so forgive them and go forward."

It's time I let go and let God take control of my life, Amelia thought. *I can't carry this burden of unforgiveness any longer. I can't take away the hurt, but God can.*

As they drove up the hollow, Amelia noticed that the creek was still running bank-full, but not the brown, muddy water of yesterday. This was dark, brackish water that rumbled ominously downstream.

"That's odd," she said to Vicky. "Rick indicated that the water was falling, and we wouldn't have any trouble. This creek is higher than it was yesterday."

"And it's a funny color, too."

"I don't like the looks of this, but there's no place to turn around, so I'll have to drive as far as the first house anyway."

The creek wasn't out of its banks yet, and Amelia stopped at the first house and blew the horn. On most trips, someone would see or hear the ERV coming and the family would be outside waiting for them. No one came in answer to the horn. They traveled on and encountered the same situation at other houses. When they reached Rosemary's home, Ashley, the oldest daughter, came out.

"What's going on? Where is everybody?" Amelia asked as she stepped out of the ERV.

"Up at the head of the hollow. There's an old slurry pond up there, and it's started leaking. Most everyone went to sandbag the leak to keep it from getting any bigger. They've been working all night. Mom wouldn't let me go—she said Jordan and I were better off here, so she wouldn't have to look out for us. I couldn't sleep, though. I was afraid the water would come up again and drown us."

"Should we go and see what we can do?" Vicky said.

Amelia shook her head. "I don't think so. If there's any chance of that dam breaking, I want to get the ERV out of here. We can't lose another one of these vehicles." To Ashley, she said, "Is there anything you need? Or any of your neighbors? Mr. Smith of the Red Cross wanted us to see if electric power and telephone service have been restored. If you can tell us that, we'll go back to headquarters and report this situation."

"We have electricity, but no phones yet."

"Then if you have no phones, we'll need to send help," Vicky said.

"Are you sure you'll be all right?" Amelia asked.

"I reckon so. I don't know what could hurt us, but I'm kinda mad at Mama for making us stay here," Ashley said. "There's a television man up at the dam taking pictures. He just happened to be here interviewing people when the black water started coming. I'd like to be on television sometime, and he might have taken my picture if I was helping with the dike."

Amelia looked around the hollow, noting that the creek bed was full and inching quickly out of its banks. "I don't want to leave you and Jordan alone. If the water does get higher before your parents return, I suppose you could climb the mountain."

"Yes. That's what Mama told us to do. That's where we stayed when the big flood came."

Vicky gave Ashley several cartons of juice and some apples, while Amelia turned the ERV around. For a woman who, until a few days ago, had never driven anything except regular cars, it was no small task to turn the vehicle. They waved goodbye to Ashley, who was going back inside with the food Vicky had given to her.

Amelia admitted that Rosemary had raised good kids, because the two girls had been polite the other time Amelia had encountered them. She looked in the rearview mirror and stopped abruptly. Ashley was running down the road behind them, waving her arms.

"Wonder what she wants?" Amelia said to Vicky, who glanced through the mirror on her side.

"Something's wrong. Do you suppose that dam

has ruptured?'' Vicky said as she jumped out of the vehicle.

"Even if it has, we have to leave," Amelia shouted. "Vicky, we can't be stranded here!"

Vicky paid her no heed and started running toward the house. Quickly, Amelia assessed the road. She had stopped on the highest spot in the hollow, which was the safest place she could find to leave the vehicle. Black water spread from hill to hill, but the road wasn't covered. She didn't want to lose the ERV, but she knew that people were more important than vehicles. She turned off the engine and ran toward Vicky and Ashley.

"Help! Jordan's gonna drown," Ashley screamed. The girl started running toward the house, with Vicky and Amelia at her heels. Ashley bypassed the house and ran toward the creek. The scene before them brought terror to Amelia's heart, and she muttered, "Oh, no."

Jordan had apparently crossed the creek on the small footbridge, but now water had covered the bridge until only the railings were visible. The child was marooned on the opposite bank, underneath a rock ledge, and the brackish water was inching closer to her.

"She's got a playhouse over there," Ashley said. "I didn't know she'd left the house. Mama will whip me for letting her out of my sight."

"Ashley," Amelia said, "run as fast as you can

and get your parents.'' Wide-eyed, Ashley only
paused a few seconds before she started racing up
the hollow.

Keeping her eyes on the crying child, Amelia
called, ''Stay where you are, Jordan. I'll come and
get you.''

Chapter Fifteen

Amelia pulled off her jacket and handed it to Vicky. She rolled the legs of her jeans to her knees. She untied her heavy boots and cast them aside. She felt momentary panic, and her stomach tightened until she felt physically sick.

Staring at the whirling waves of black sludge edging upward toward them, Vicky said, "You can't swim in that. Wait until help comes."

"We don't know how long it will take for her parents to arrive." With the memory of Chase's near escape in her mind, she added, "I can't stand here and watch her die." She prayed for strength and the will to steady her erratic pulse. Momentarily, she sensed the agony she'd experienced a few days earlier when she feared Chase would drown.

"If you have trouble, I can't help you," Vicky

persisted. "I can't swim a lick. Wait, Amelia. It shouldn't be too long before her parents get here."

"I don't know how far away that pond is. Her parents might not make it in time. The water has risen several inches since we came here fifteen minutes ago."

Normally, the shallow creek bed wasn't more than twenty feet across, but it was wider than that now, and she couldn't determine the depth.

Amelia twisted her long hair behind her head and secured it with an elastic band from her pocket. Taking a deep breath, she walked to the edge of the water.

"If I could only help," Vicky wailed.

"You can pray that I'll have the strength and wisdom to save this child."

Amelia stepped gingerly into the brackish water that felt as thick as mud. Her feet slid, but she caught herself before she fell. She waded cautiously until there was suddenly no more ground beneath her feet. She'd left the bank and was in the creek bed. The current was much swifter in the deeper water, and it swept Amelia's feet from under her. Her head submerged completely, and the pressure of the water rolled her over. She struggled to keep from being pulled downstream.

She kicked to the surface, conscious that her hair was falling over her face. She shook her head to clear her eyes of the brackish water. Jordan, still clutching her doll, stood at the edge of the water.

"I'm coming, Jordan!" she called. "Stay where you are."

With powerful reaching strokes, she drove through the flood that flung itself at her like a moving wall. She discounted any danger to herself, intent only on reaching that little patch of earth, which looked as if it was getting smaller by the second. After that admonition to Jordan, Amelia closed her mouth tightly to keep from swallowing any of the polluted, foul-smelling water.

The force of the water strained her body, and although she'd once been a good swimmer, she hadn't kept in practice. She shook away a momentary weakness and steadied herself.

God, help me, she prayed. *I don't have the strength to do this alone.*

"Amelia!" she heard Vicky shout. "Watch that tree."

She looked quickly to her right and saw the tree limb bearing down on her rapidly. Praying that there weren't a lot of branches beneath the water, she dived hurriedly and lunged underneath the water in the general direction of the place where Jordan stood. When Amelia surfaced, the limb was below her, but she could scarcely breathe. She set her teeth and slowly fought toward the bank. When her feet touched a gravel bar, she knew she was close to the child.

Breathing deeply, Amelia collapsed on the ground for a moment to catch her breath. Jordan stumbled toward her, big tears flooding her eyes.

Amelia hugged the girl to her. "Don't worry, honey. I'll take you to your parents soon."

Amelia's socks were soaked with water, and her wet jeans felt like straitjackets around her legs. Even if it was only a short distance to travel, the water was swift, and with a child on her back, she needed all the freedom of movement she could muster.

Thankful that only Vicky would be watching, between gasping breaths, Amelia removed her socks and jeans. Her flannel shirt clung to her body, barely covering her cotton panties, but she knew this was no time for modesty. She twisted her hair into a roll and pushed it over her shoulder. An uneasy glance at the water told her she had to hurry.

"Does your daddy ever ride you piggyback?" she asked Jordan.

"Uh-huh!" Jordan nodded emphatically.

"Then that's what you'll have to do now. Wrap your arms around my neck and lock them together. Put your legs around my waist. Don't let go, no matter what happens—even if our heads go under the water, hold your breath and hold on to me. Just pretend it's a game and let me worry about the water. Can you do that?"

"Yes. What about Dolly?" she asked.

Amelia knew that Jordan would be more relaxed if her dolly was safe, but there wasn't any way she could carry the doll. Aware that the water lapped at her feet, she said, "Let's see if we can find a place for Dolly."

She stood on unsteady legs and looked around the area. A few inches above her head, a small tree extended from a crevice in the rock cliff.

"Let's put Dolly up on this tree, so she can watch as we swim across the water."

Jordan relinquished the doll, and Amelia put it astraddle of the tree trunk. Then she hunkered down on the ground. "Come on, Jordan. Climb on my back."

Jordan's little arms gripped Amelia's neck and nearly choked her. "Not that tight, honey." The child's hold loosened, and Amelia tucked the child's legs around her waist.

"Hug me with your legs," she said, and Jordan's knees clenched Amelia's midriff.

"Hold on. No matter what happens, don't let go." Amelia stood and eased slowly into the water. As she looked toward Vicky to get her bearings, Amelia saw several people running toward the creek. She recognized Rosemary.

Momentarily, Amelia thought, That woman wrecked my home, and I'm risking my life to save her daughter. What irony!

A man ran beside Rosemary, whom Amelia supposed to be her husband. "I'll come after her," he shouted.

Rosemary grabbed him. "You've got a broken arm," she shouted in agitation. "You can't go out there,"

"Wait!" Amelia shouted across the roaring water. "I'll make it—just be ready to grab her from my back when I get close enough."

The gravelly ground stung Amelia's feet as she eased toward the deeper water, but without her socks and jeans, she felt more in command of her movements. And her mind eased, knowing that there were others now on the bank, who could probably save Jordan if she faltered. When she reached out a foot and knew she was at the creek bed, she said to Jordan, "Hold on, honey, here we go."

Jordan squealed when the water covered her feet and lower body, but her little arms and legs tightened instinctively around Amelia's body.

As Amelia shot out into the creek, a wave rolled over her, and she was wrenched sideways by the current. But, breathing deeply, she treaded water steadily. More than halfway across, fear gripped her, and Amelia's heart stirred with fright and weakness. She halted momentarily and closed her eyes. Knowing how much depended on her, and fighting the current with all of her strength, she opened her eyes and focused on Vicky. The spectators shouted encouragement, and the nearer she came to the bank, the louder they called, almost as if she was playing in a sporting event. But the unusual exertion undermined her strength, and there were times when Amelia doubted she could make it. She thought of Chase, and how he'd mourn if she drowned. That thought kept her weary arms reaching forward, and at last, a torrent swept her against the opposite bank.

Amelia stumbled when her feet struck ground, but she recovered her stride and trudged up the remaining few feet. Amelia turned so Jordan's father could pull the child from her back. Relieved of the burden of Jordan's body, she lifted her head and saw that she was looking into the lens of a TV camera. Suddenly realizing that she'd left most of her clothes on the other side of the creek, she stretched her wet shirt to cover as much of her body as she could.

Vicky put her arms around Amelia's waist, and Amelia welcomed the shield to her near-nudity, thankful that the long shirttail covered her thighs. "That's the bravest thing I've ever seen anyone do," Vicky said between sobs.

"Yes, it was, ma'am," the TV reporter at her side said, holding a microphone under her nose. "Why'd you do it?"

Pushing the mass of her wet hair away from her face, Amelia answered, "What else could I do? The child needed saving, and I was the only adult here who could swim."

She turned and looked toward the creek. The place where Jordan had been stranded was now covered with the blackish slurry. Rosemary and her family were still trying to calm Jordan, who'd become hysterical now that the danger was over.

"Let's get out of here," Amelia said.

"Are you hurt?" Vicky asked.

"I don't know, but I've got to get the Red Cross ERV out of this hollow before the road is blocked. And I don't want any more attention. Come on, Vicky." She grabbed her jacket off the ground and wrapped it around her waist and headed toward the ERV. The television man trotted at her heels, hammering questions at her, which she ignored. She was aware that the cameraman was documenting her every move.

"What size shoes do you wear, Vicky?"

"Seven."

"Then let me have them. I can't drive in my bare feet."

When they got to the ERV, Vicky took off her shoes and handed them to Amelia. While Amelia tried on the shoes, a size too big for her, Vicky spread a blanket over the driver's seat.

"When can I interview you, ma'am?" the reporter said. "You've just saved a child's life. I want a story."

"I told you, I did what I had to do. I'm thankful

the little girl is safe. Please! I don't want any notoriety.''

Suddenly feeling weak, it was all she could do to step into the vehicle.

As they started out of the hollow, Vicky glanced at her watch. "It's only been a half hour since we started to leave the first time." She laughed nervously. Looking at Amelia, she said, "Aren't you even frightened? I'm shaking all over."

"I haven't had time to get scared. Once we get back to Williamson, and I hand this vehicle over to Rick, I figure I'll be shaking, too."

Amelia was as tense as a bowstring until she cleared the hollow before any of the road was covered with water. Then nervous reaction took over. Her foot started to shake on the accelerator when they reached the paved highway, and she knew she really shouldn't be driving. By the time she drove the ERV into the parking lot at Mountainview Church, her mouth was dry, her hands were shaking and her eyes bleary. Perhaps aware of the strain Amelia was under, most of the time, Vicky sat wordlessly beside her.

When she slowed the ERV to a halt and turned off the ignition, she muttered, "Thank You, God, for Your help today, but please deliver me from enduring another experience like that." Her head slumped forward on the steering wheel.

Vicky gasped. "Have you fainted?"

"No, I'm just exhausted. I'll be all right as soon as I catch my breath."

"Here comes Rick," Vicky said.

Rick opened the door on the driver's side, and Amelia looked up.

"What else is going to happen to you?" he said.

"You know?"

"We've been glued to the TV watching you rescue that child."

"That was a live broadcast?" Amelia gasped.

"Yes. The reporter was from a national network, so your rescue will probably hit the evening news."

Peering between strands of sodden hair that screened her face, Amelia said, "My first time on national TV, and I had to be half-naked, looking like a drowned rat."

"Are you all right?" Rick asked.

"I think so."

"You're going to the hospital to be checked out. I'll take you in my van. If they will, I want them to admit you for observation."

"My insurance cards are in my car."

"I'll get them," Vicky said, bouncing out of the ERV and running toward Amelia's Buick.

"I really should take a shower," Amelia said. "Give me time to stop at the motel and shower, then you can pick me up."

"I'll drive you to the motel and wait until you've showered."

At first, Amelia thought that Rick was being over-cautious to insist that she see a doctor, but by the time she'd showered, dried her hair and dressed, she was nauseous. Her head hurt. Her pulse rate was weak and rapid. She felt weak and dizzy. With an effort, she walked to the exit, her head reeling as the elevator descended. When Rick saw her stumbling toward him, he jumped out of his car and helped her into the seat. She was conscious that he fastened her seat belt, but the next thing she knew she was on a hospital gurney being wheeled to the emergency room.

The next hour or so was hazy to Amelia as she was turned, tossed, stuck with needles and discussed by medics and nurses. She was partly conscious when she heard a nurse say, "We can't find any serious problems. It's mostly exhaustion and shock, a reaction to her experience. The doctor wants to admit her for observation."

The next thing she remembered, Amelia was awakened by an aide with her dinner tray.

"Feeling better?" the woman asked.

Groggily, Amelia said, "I'm not sure."

The woman placed the tray on the bedside table and uncovered it.

"Soup, crackers and yogurt tonight, but you can have a regular meal tomorrow. Are you hungry?"

Amelia pushed the button and raised the head of

her bed. "Not really, but I don't feel sick to my stomach now."

The aide pointed to an IV bag hanging behind the bed. "You're getting medicine for that."

Amelia was in a private room, which suited her mood for the present. Her hand shook as she picked up the spoon. As she sipped on the mild broth, she realized she was still trembling inwardly, too.

She'd had a narrow escape. In the past, when her life had felt empty, she would have welcomed death. But today, not only had she been fighting to save Jordan's life, she hadn't wanted to die, either. She believed that was because of her reunion with Chase. If she and Chase did reunite, she had more to live for now.

The aide had turned on the television hanging from the wall, and when Amelia noticed a familiar scene, she increased the volume. Was that the creek behind Rosemary's property? It appeared that a seal was moving against the current until the cameraman zoomed closer. As Amelia feared, it was a live picture of her swimming with Jordan hanging on her back.

"Many acts of heroism have been witnessed during the tragic floods now devastating southern West Virginia," the anchorwoman said. "Today brought another example of heroism when Amelia Stone, a Red Cross volunteer, jumped unaided into a rapidly rising stream of coal slurry, escaping from a rift in an abandoned pond, to rescue a four-year-old child.''

Horrified, Amelia watched as the camera caught her stepping from the water. From head to toe she was smeared with the thick, black mud. Her flannel shirt twisted around her waist, partially covering her thighs. Irritated, Amelia muttered, ''Indecent expo sure on national television.''

''Why'd you do it?'' she saw the newsman ask.

A replay of her words sounded arrogant. ''What else could I do? The child needed saving, and I was the only adult here who could swim.''

But how could she have given a sensible answer after that harrowing experience? There followed a picture of her rushing to the ERV, changing into Vicky's shoes, and their rapid departure from the hollow. Disgusted, Amelia turned off the television, pushed the tray away, lowered the bed and sulked.

She'd never been a person to call attention to herself, and she didn't relish the position of being in the spotlight. She turned on her side and dozed until the nurse came to check her vitals.

''How are you feeling?''

''Rocky. I'm still trembling inside, and my muscles are letting me know I haven't been swimming for a long time. I ache all over.''

''A good night's sleep will do wonders for you,'' the nurse assured her. As she checked Amelia's blood pressure, she continued. "I see you made the evening news."

Amelia groaned. "Yes, my only day in the limelight, and I surely made a spectacle of myself. When I took off my jeans, I didn't know the whole nation would be looking."

The nurse, who was a bit on the hefty side, said, "If I had legs like yours, I wouldn't care who saw them."

"Covered with that black slime, they didn't look very attractive to me. It was my bad luck that there was a newsman on the spot."

"Oh, enjoy the publicity while it lasts. Praise doesn't come our way very often."

"I don't need that kind of praise. I'd just as soon not be reminded of this morning. I'll probably have bad dreams for years about drowning."

"I've checked on you several times, and you've been muttering in your sleep. But you'll soon forget the danger and be happy that you were able to save the little girl's life."

"Did they bring her to the hospital, too? I should have stayed to check on her, but I was too intent on getting the Red Cross vehicle out of that hollow."

"They didn't bring her to this hospital. Apparently, they thought there wasn't any need."

"I probably wouldn't have needed to come either if I hadn't had to drive the ERV back to headquarters. That tested my strength more than the rescue did.''

''We've had several local reporters wanting to talk to you, but the doctor posted a No Visitors sign on your door.''

''Thank him for me. I don't want any visitors.''

''The doctor wants you to have some rest before he releases you.''

''Good. I feel as if I could sleep for a week.''

''I'll turn out the light.''

Amelia wasn't sleepy, but she closed her eyes. Had she been in danger of losing her life? She relived the few minutes she'd spent rescuing Jordan. When her head had suddenly gone underwater, that could have been dangerous if she hadn't kept her wits about her. As she'd dived when the tree limb was heading toward her, she could have been knocked unconscious. Yes, many things could have happened, but she hadn't even considered the danger.

''Yea, though I walk through the valley of the shadow of death, I will fear no evil,'' the psalmist had said. Probably she had been in the valley of death, but she hadn't been afraid. Why not? Was it because she didn't have anything to live for?

A few weeks ago she might have thought that, but now that Chase had reentered her life, she'd started contemplating life on earth with greater anticipation than she'd ever done before. She wanted more time with Chase, but she honestly believed, if she had died, that eternity in the presence of God far superseded the fleeting pleasures of life on earth. Paul, the apostle, had said, "I am torn between the two: I desire to depart and be with Christ, which is far better; but it is more necessary for you that I remain in the body."

Apparently, God wasn't ready for her yet, and if not, He still had a purpose for her on earth. She believed God had indeed given her and Chase a second chance for love, and that's the reason she hadn't perished in the flood.

Amelia eased into a light sleep, aware each time one of the staff checked on her through the night. So when the door opened about daylight, she assumed it was another nurse. She lay on her side, facing the door, and she opened her eyes, unprepared for the face that peered in.

"Chase! I thought you were in Ohio."

"Shhh!" he said with a grin. "I sneaked past the nurse's station, after I was told you weren't allowed any visitors."

"How did you hear?"

"Vicky called as soon as they admitted you to the hospital yesterday. I wasn't at the bank, so she called my apartment and left a message on the answering machine. But I'd already seen the rescue on the evening news in a restaurant before I went home." He leaned over her and swept a soft kiss on her lips, then pulled a chair close to the bed where he could hold her hand that didn't have an IV attached.

"But shouldn't you be at work? You're going to get fired."

"I cleared it with the bank's president, and told him to debit my salary. He refused, but I'll make it up some way. Are you getting along all right?"

Her stiff neck hindered her slight nod. "I'm okay, but I do have lots of sore places, and I feel drained. I haven't been up yet, but my legs feel as limp as spaghetti."

"You shouldn't have taken such a risk."

"Would you have stood aside, done nothing, and watched a child die?"

"No."

"Of course, you wouldn't, and neither could I."

He squeezed her fingers gently. "I know you did the only thing possible, but every mile coming down here seemed like twenty. I had to see for myself that you were still alive."

"Thanks, Chase. I think the doctor will release me today." She hesitated a bit before saying, "Do you know who the girl was?"

"No. I was so dumbfounded when I saw you and learned what you'd done that I missed the name of the child. Who was she?"

"Jordan." When she noted that the name didn't

signify anything to him, she said, "Rosemary's daughter."

He stared at her in amazement. "Oh, poor Amelia! What a choice you had to make."

"You underestimate me, Chase. There wasn't any choice."

"Oh, sweetheart, I shouldn't have said that. I know you well enough to realize that you wouldn't hesitate." He lifted her hand to his lips and kissed her palm. "I can't thank God enough that He left you with me instead of taking you home to be with Him. He's spared us a few more years—let's take advantage of them."

"I'm too vulnerable now to make a lifetime commitment, but I'm mostly sure that's what I want to do."

"If this accident influenced your decision, I'm almost glad that it happened. Now, I'm going to sneak out of here, go find a room and get some sleep. I drove all night."

Cupping his hands around her face, Chase stooped and kissed her, a slow, tender kiss that held a promise.

After the doctor reported that all of her vitals were great, and the nurse disconnected the IV, Amelia took a shower, washed her hair and felt much better. Even though she'd showered and shampooed her hair at the motel yesterday, the stench of the murky water remained in her nostrils. She relaxed on the bed, thinking dreamily of the future awaiting her and Chase.

Her thoughts were somewhat troubled, though. If they remarried, would she move or would Chase? She would be the logical one to move because she could probably find a position with the American Red Cross in any major city. And she wouldn't mind, because she had many acquaintances, but few close friends, in Philadelphia. After yesterday's experience, when she could have lost her life, minor things seemed to have passed into the background. Despite the trouble Rosemary had caused her, she was thankful that she'd had an opportunity to save Jordan. When she remembered the trauma she'd experienced after she'd miscarried, she could imagine what it would have been like for Rosemary to have lost a child she'd had four years. Amelia wouldn't have wished that on her worst enemy, and that's what she'd considered Rosemary for many years.

Amelia was half-asleep when the door opened again, and for a moment she hardly recognized the well-dressed couple who entered the room.

"Amelia," Pauline Stone cried, rushing to the bed to clutch her daughter's hand. "Are you all right?"

Amelia sat up in bed and accepted her mother's embrace. She glanced toward her father, surprised to note that he had tears in his eyes, and his lips were quivering. She reached her hand to him, and he squeezed it tightly.

"Of course, I'm all right. How did you know? I thought you were on a cruise."

"We were on a cruise," Alex said, "but the ship does have TVs, you know. We saw the report on the news when the ship was in port, and we caught a plane to the mainland immediately."

"Whatever made you take such a risk, Amelia?" her mother scolded.

"Now, Pauline," Alex said, "you know she's always been like that—remember that time she jumped in our swimming pool to rescue a cat?"

"Well, she wasn't old enough to know better then," Pauline said. "When are you going to be released from the hospital?"

"Sometime today."

"We've come to take you home with us."

The tenderness in her mother's voice amazed Amelia, and she was barely able to suppress her gasp of surprise.

"Oh, return to your cruise. I'm going back to work as soon as I'm released. I have two more days on this assignment."

"Please, Amelia," Pauline said, and she started crying. "We didn't realize how much we loved you until we saw that you could have lost your life. I know we haven't been the devoted parents we should have been, and we've missed an important part of your life. Give us another chance. Come home with us and let us look after you.''

So she and Chase weren't the only ones to be given a second chance at love!

''I really don't need anyone to look after me, Mother. I'll come for a visit soon, but I can't leave the work undone here. I want to complete my assignment. If you've looked around, you see how badly volunteers are needed.''

''We saw a lot of the damage as we drove from the Charleston airport,'' Alex said. ''It's the most desolate country I've ever seen. Even in good times, this couldn't be a pleasant place to live.''

If being a dutiful daughter meant agreeing with all of her parents' biases, she couldn't conform. Her parents had never been in sympathy with her Christian views. Perhaps now that they were mellowing, she would be able to influence them, so she spoke cautiously.

''No, Dad, it isn't desolate. This month I've met some of the most wonderful people I've ever known. Not only the hundreds of volunteers who've come from all over the United States to help, but the natives are great. It's remarkable how they bounce back after such a disaster. It's been a privilege for me to serve here.''

Pauline shook her head slowly. ''We've never understood you, Amelia.''

Once this would have ruffled Amelia's feathers,

but she leaned over and kissed her mother's cheek. "Then don't try to understand me. Just love me the way I am."

"We do," Alex said. "Even if you won't go home with us, we're still going to stay until you're discharged."

"You probably can't find a motel room. Most of the motels are filled with volunteers, but there might be accommodations across the river in Kentucky."

"We'll look around and see what we can find. Bye for now," her mother said, and leaned over to kiss Amelia's forehead.

Amelia lay with her eyes closed, contemplating the strange about-face of her parents. If she'd thought about the situation, she'd have expected her mother to throw a fit because Amelia had removed most of her clothes in public. She prayed that her parents' change of heart wasn't temporary. A faint smile played across Amelia's face when she considered how nice it would be to have a real family like other people. If Chase and she remarried, and her parents really did want her to come home, perhaps she could enjoy the closeness of family holidays like other people did.

Chapter Sixteen

Amelia hadn't heard anything, but she sensed a presence in the room and opened her eyes. Rosemary stood by the bed, strange emotions playing across her face. Amelia was amazed to see this visitor, too, and she was thankful Rosemary hadn't shown up while her parents were in the room.

Motioning to the chair her mother had recently vacated, Amelia said, "Sit down."

Rosemary perched uneasily on the edge of the chair.

"Thanks for saving Jordan's life," she said quickly. "My husband wanted to come with me to thank you, too, but I needed to talk to you alone today. I can't believe, after the way I treated you, that you'd actually save my daughter's life. If the situation had been reversed, I'm not sure I would have done the same for you."

"I'm thankful that God allowed me to be there to rescue Jordan. You and your husband would probably have gotten there in time to save her, but I couldn't risk it."

Rosemary shook her head. "I doubt it. I think Ashley would have tried to save her sister and both of them would have died. She said you sent her to get us. I haven't slept a wink since it happened, thinking of what might have been. I have lots of faults, but I do love my children."

Impulsively, Amelia took Rosemary's hand. "I can understand how you feel." She felt compelled to tell Rosemary what very few people knew—neither her mother and father nor Chase's parents. "I had a miscarriage several years ago. I've never forgotten the emotional pain involved, after only a few months of pregnancy. I can only imagine how horrible it would be to lose a child you've nurtured and loved for years. I've always felt so bereft because I don't have any children."

A look of pain crossed Rosemary's face. "Which you might have had if I hadn't meddled in your life."

"That may be, but I may just be one of those women who can't bear children. I had a hysterectomy a few years ago."

"Well, regardless, I ruined your marriage. After what you've done for me, I feel downright guilty to have three children, as well as a husband who's good to me.''

''Don't be. I'm not jealous of other women who have children. I'm glad you have a nice family. I've always felt guilty, too, when it seemed you blamed me for ruining your relationship with Chase.''

''I hated you for that, Rosemary admitted ''That's the reason I deliberately set out to break up your marriage. But because of what you've done for me, I'm going to level with you. I took that job where Chase worked, and I made plenty of advances, but he ignored them. Then when we went on that business trip together, I had the feeling that things weren't going well between the two of you.''

Momentarily, hatred welled up inside Amelia. Naturally, things weren't going well for her and Chase— she'd just lost their baby. How dare Rosemary take advantage of a time when Chase was unhappy! But she was determined she wouldn't allow her resentment to prevent a forgiving attitude toward Rosemary.

Not meeting Amelia's eyes, Rosemary continued, speaking rapidly, as if she was eager to divest her conscience of the guilt she carried. ''I poured water in my gas tank to make it malfunction. Chase tried to call you, and when you didn't answer, I turned on all the charm I had. I was the one to suggest that we take only one room, but Chase didn't object. The next day, he was definitely sorry. He told me on the way home that he loved you and that there couldn't be anything else between us.''

Amelia felt her anger rising, not only at Rosemary, but also at herself, for not giving Chase the benefit of a doubt. ''So I was too hasty in divorcing him?''

''I dropped a few hints to people and the gossip started. After you turned from him, Chase and I were together a few times, but he couldn't forget you. I lost again.''

''But why, Rosemary? I didn't really take Chase away from you, as you said. He was dating other people the same time he was dating you. I didn't go out with him the first time he asked me. Why?''

''Because I'm a bitter person, I suppose. I had an abusive childhood—physically and sexually. Even when I grew older, it seemed as if I attracted the wrong kind of man. Chase was the first guy who treated me like a lady. Yes, he dated other people, but he wasn't serious about any of them, and I hoped I could win him. I don't know whether I loved him, but he was such a nice person, and I wanted him. I thought we were on the verge of a commitment until he started dating you, and after that, he didn't have eyes for anyone else. I had nothing against you personally. I'd have felt the same way about anyone he married. I don't expect you to forgive me, but I am sorry for the trouble I caused you.''

"But I do forgive you, and I thank you for telling me the truth."

"Are Chase and you going back together?"

"Yes, I think so."

"That makes me feel a little better, but I'm still ashamed of myself."

"I hope you're happy now, Rosemary. Your girls are adorable."

"I'm *not* unhappy, and my husband is good to me, but something is still missing."

Amelia had always been reluctant to openly witness to others about her faith, but somehow she felt compelled to say, "I felt the same way for a year after Chase and I divorced, but I went to a counselor who convinced me that my greatest needs were spiritual. My heart was filled with anger against you and Chase for months, until I realized healing wouldn't come until I released that anger."

"I still don't know how you could forgive me."

Amelia reached for the Gideon Bible on the table beside her bed. "The answer is in here," she said. She turned to the book of Colossians in the New Testament. "Here's a verse that I read over and over until the message was seared into my mind and heart. 'Bear with each other and whatever grievances you may have against one another. Forgive as the Lord forgave you.'"

"Pretty words," Rosemary said cynically, "but weren't they hard to put into practice?"

"At first, yes, but to have the peace I wanted, forgiveness had to come. After I met Chase again, and we encountered you, I realized that I hadn't forgiven as completely as I'd hoped. This month, I've lived the pain of Chase's rejection over and over again, but after my near-death experience yesterday, I believe that at last, the slate has been wiped clean."

"Should I tell my husband about my past? I feel guilty living with him when he doesn't know about me."

Amelia considered this for a few minutes. She didn't feel competent in the role of a marriage counselor. "At the moment, I can't think of any Scripture verse to answer your question, but I'll give my opinion. You've lived with your husband several years now, and you've had his children. I can't see any reason for making him and the children miserable just so you can wipe out your personal guilt. Ask God to forgive you of what you did in the past. He'll forgive you, but I don't believe He'd expect you to unload the full burden of your mistake on your husband."

Even as she talked to Rosemary, Amelia could see many parallels in her own need to completely forgive and forget the past.

"When I started going to church, I found the peace I needed in the Bible and from the encouragement of other Christians. Since our divorce, both

Chase and I have accepted Jesus into our lives. We both believe that mutual commitment has given us the foundation for a good marriage. I've been hesitating about marrying again because I was afraid I'd never fully forget what Chase had done, but your coming has made it so much easier. I encourage you to go to church, start reading the Bible and let God work the same miracle in your life that He has in mine.''

Amelia swung her feet over the side of the bed and reached for Rosemary, who fell into her arms, crying.

"Thanks, Amelia,'' she sobbed. "I don't deserve your forgiveness, let alone God's, but I'll try. I can't bear the burden of my mistakes any longer.''

Chase walked in and found them in each other's arms. He drew a quick, sharp breath. When Rosemary looked up and saw Chase, she bolted out of the chair and ran from the room. Chase stood aside to let her pass by him. Noting the ludicrous look on his face, Amelia's lips quivered with mirth.

"You'll never believe what's been going on here today.''

Chase couldn't remember that he'd ever seen Amelia so alive and vibrant. He hurried to her bedside and clasped the hand she held out to him.

"Tell me.''

"My parents saw Jordan's rescue on television yesterday. They left their Caribbean cruise and came home. They were in here earlier today. Mother wants to take me home with them to recuperate."

"Are you going?"

She shook her head. "I told them I'd come for a visit, but I'm not an invalid. I'm all right, and I intend to work my few remaining days here. I couldn't believe they were distressed because I'd been in danger. It was quite a change."

"I'm glad for you, Melly," Chase said, and his eyes lighted with love and compassion. "I've never thought they didn't love you, but they had a poor way of showing it."

"I suppose they didn't mean to be unkind, but they're so devoted to each other, they didn't need anyone else to bring them happiness. I'm urging them to return to their cruise, and I'll visit them after they're back at Hilton Head. I don't need to recuperate, but it should make Mother feel better if she can fuss over me for a few days."

It was Chase's opinion that Amelia was overdue for some coddling from her mother.

"Do you want to tell me about Rosemary?"

"Yes, because it affects you, too. Since I'd saved her daughter's life, she said she owed me. She admitted that she deliberately set out to ruin our marriage." Rosemary hadn't told her to keep secret the details of her revelation, and Amelia told him everything.

"And, Chase," she concluded, "I feel terrible

that I didn't meet you halfway when you asked me to forgive you. If I hadn't been so unforgiving, we would have had fifteen years of happiness. Perhaps we could have had children. It's all my fault. I should have realized you were hurt over losing our child, too. I was too wrapped up in my own sorrow to see how much we needed each other.''

"The past is gone! We'll build our future on our previous mistakes.''

A nurse interrupted them. "The doctor says you can be released, Miss Stone. We'll have your papers ready in an hour.''

"I'll wait in the lobby until you're ready to go," Chase said.

After she showered and dressed in the clothes that Vicky had brought from their room earlier that day, Amelia scrutinized her features carefully as she applied some makeup. She did look rather peaked, and an uncertainty crept into her expression. Something flickered far back in her eyes, and she wondered if it was fear. If she developed a closer relationship with her parents and Chase, and they married again, her whole life would undergo a flip-flop. Was she emotionally ready for such a drastic change of lifestyle?

She was forty-three, and until she'd encountered Chase three weeks ago, she'd been reconciled to her way of life. Should she leave well enough alone? Wasn't it enough that she no longer harbored any ill will against her parents, Chase or Rosemary? Did she fear getting hurt again? Had his infidelity ruined her for another close relationship, even with Chase?

Oh, God. Why do I continue to have these doubts?

When her parents returned, Pauline said, "You look much better. We can't find a motel, and if you're sure you won't go home with us, we will return to the cruise ship. We left in such a hurry, we didn't bring all of our luggage."

"I'm pleased you came to see about me, but I'd rather you'd finish your vacation. I'll stay here a few more days and then return to Philadelphia. After you get home, call me and we'll arrange a time for me to visit."

"Our plane leaves Yeager Airport about nine o'clock tonight, so we have time to take you to dinner."

"I'll be ready as soon as the nurse arrives with papers for me to sign. Do you mind if Chase comes with us? He came early this morning, and he's waiting in the lobby."

"Of course, we don't mind. We want to see him," Pauline said. Alex's face broadened into a smile. They'd always been fond of Chase and had treated him like a son. Would their attitude toward her have been different if she'd been a *boy?* Those were answers to questions she'd never ask so Amelia determined to put them out of her mind.

When Chase strolled in, she witnessed a joyful reunion between him and her parents. Seeing their pleasure, Amelia was briefly assailed with another pang of guilt. By her stubbornness, she'd caused their separation, too.

They went to the Brass Tree Restaurant to eat, and after they'd ordered, Pauline Stone said happily, "It's amazing to see the two of you together again. We've always been sorry about your divorce. Since you seem so friendly now, are you going to marry again?"

Chase looked toward Amelia for the answer. He was ready, but he had to wait for her definite answer.

"I think so," Amelia said slowly, "even if I still have a few reservations."

"What reservations?" Alex Stone said. "Neither of you has remarried, and you still love each other. That's obvious. We could never understand why you divorced in the first place."

"I'm going to tell you what caused our divorce," Chase said, "since Amelia wouldn't tell you."

"Chase, please. It doesn't matter now."

His hand closed over hers. "It matters to me." Looking Alex straight in the eye, he said, "I was unfaithful to Amelia. She had a right to divorce me."

While her parents looked stunned, Amelia jumped to his defense. "But I should have forgiven you, regardless of the circumstances."

Still holding Amelia's hand, he said, "I'm ready to marry her, but Amelia needs a little more time to be sure. I assume we'll have your blessing on another marriage."

"Well, of course. We've missed having you in the family," Pauline said. "We intend to be more devoted parents to Amelia, and we want to include you in our family circle again."

"The years make a difference in all of our attitudes," Alex Stone said. "At first, I couldn't understand why Amelia would want to work in a situation like this. Now that I've witnessed the destruction, the havoc in the lives of these residents and their determination to go forward, I can see why people volunteer. I wish there was something I could do."

Apparently her parents hadn't received her letter to them before they'd left on the cruise. "There is something you can do," Amelia said. She explained about the ERV accident that had almost taken Chase's life. Her parents quickly agreed to contribute enough money to replace the vehicle.

After her parents left, intending to fly to the Caribbean and complete their cruise, Amelia and Chase drove to the Mountainview Church to check in with Rick Smith.

"Just wanted you to know that I've been released from the hospital and am ready to return to work,"

Amelia said. "I have two days to fulfill my agreement."

"What about you, Chase?"

"I'm going home tomorrow so I can be at the bank on Monday. It's been a pleasure working with you, Rick."

He looked from Chase to Amelia and back again. "I still can't figure you two out."

Chase laughed, and when he looked at Amelia, she nodded her approval.

"We were married twenty years ago, but we've been divorced for fifteen years. We're so thankful that God brought us together and gave us a second chance."

"So you're going to be man and wife again?"

Rick was called to the telephone before they answered.

Chapter Seventeen

Amelia and Chase followed Rick into the church basement. After a brief conversation, Rick handed the phone to Chase.

"It's a message for you and Amelia," he said.

Chase held the receiver so Amelia could hear.

The caller identified himself as one of the Newberrys' neighbors. "Josh had a heart attack yesterday and died before we could get him to the hospital," the man said. "An ambulance couldn't get up the hollow. Mandy wanted me to let you know that the funeral will be tomorrow morning at ten."

"Oh, that's so sad," Amelia answered him. "We'll come to the funeral."

"Don't forget the bridge washed out," the man said. "You can't drive up the hollow."

As if Amelia would ever forget about that bridge collapse where Chase almost lost his life!

"Where will the funeral be?" Chase asked.

"At their home," the man said. "There's a burying place on their farm."

"Tell Mandy we'll be praying for her and hope to see her tomorrow," Amelia said.

"We've put up a swinging bridge so you can walk in and out," the man said.

"Thanks for letting us know. We'll be there," Chase said, and handed the phone back to Rick.

"Will this delay your return to Ohio?" Amelia asked as they walked away from the church.

"I'll go home right after the funeral, and be ready to work on Monday."

The creek was no longer flooding, but Amelia's hands twisted into fists of distress the next morning when they came in sight of the destroyed bridge where Chase had almost lost his life. A wrecker had pulled the ERV out of the water, and it had been damaged beyond repair. Amelia felt better about the situation now that she knew her parents would pay for a new vehicle.

Several cars were parked along the road, apparently cars belonging to the Newberry family and their friends. Chase had to park his truck in a very small spot, as space was limited.

As they walked along the narrow road, Amelia compared the present one to their first trip up the hollow three weeks ago. The first day, it had been drizzling rain, and they'd faced a sodden landscape. She remembered how happy Josh and Mandy had been to return home. Now, suddenly, Mandy was left alone. Considering the pathos she'd experienced in this area, Amelia felt as if these weeks were longer than the rest of her life put together.

Today, the sun shone occasionally through some intermittent clouds, but Amelia couldn't tell if they were rain clouds.

"I hope it doesn't rain on Josh's funeral," she said. "Mandy has had enough to bear during the last month."

"The meteorologist said on the morning news that it would be fair today."

When they reached the Newberry farm, Amelia reached for Chase's hand because she felt a bit out of place. At least a hundred people crowded the space between the house and the barn. Many of the faces seemed familiar. When these people nodded in their direction, Amelia figured they'd served food to them through the disaster relief. She didn't see anyone they knew by name except Mandy and her daughter Emily.

Chase nudged her, and she looked in the direction he was pointing. Willie Honaker was lumbering toward them.

"Say," he said, his black eyes gleaming, "I'm glad to see you. Since you hadn't been around my place for a while, I figgered you'd left Mingo County for good.''

A guitarist started playing, and Chase said quietly, ''We're leaving soon, but wanted to be here for this funeral.''

Willie shook their hands. ''I'm a pallbearer, so's I'll go up front. I just wanted to say that you've brought a lot of pleasure to my life.''

Amelia and Chase nodded their thanks. All the chairs were occupied. They moved to the background and leaned against a large maple tree that had shaded the Newberry home for years.

An open, inexpensive casket was placed on the porch, and even at a distance Amelia saw Josh's features resembling the face of his youngest son, more than the wrinkled, rough skin of the man Amelia had known. At least thirty members of Josh's immediate family sat on folding chairs, facing the casket. The boys had the stalwart physique of their father, and most of them had blond hair as both Mandy and Josh must have had in their youth. Emily turned, noted the presence of Amelia and Chase and waved to them.

The preacher stepped up on the porch and prayed, then a male quartet accompanied by a guitarist sang ''Will the Circle Be Unbroken?'' a song Amelia had never heard. The lyrics were sad, and Amelia's throat constricted with unshed tears. The five verses of the song dealt with the tender days of childhood in an earthly home, and the happiness the family had enjoyed around the fireside. Amelia didn't know how Mandy could control her grief. One of the verses mentioned how the family circle had been broken when the children went away one by one, but the family would be reunited in heaven someday.

Although Amelia's heart grieved for the loss of her newly-found friend, she noted that Mandy listened to the song with a smile on her face. No doubt, her main comfort came from the conclusion of the song that said a better home awaited the departed one.

Amelia's gaze roved around the barren homesite. As she had on the first day she'd been here, she thought what a miserable place it was to live. In her opinion, Josh hadn't had a good house here on earth, and it gave her comfort to believe that he had gone to a better home.

Amelia had avoided funerals whenever possible, but at most of the funerals she'd attended the minister had read portions of the twenty-third Psalm. Today, the preacher used the psalmist illustration of God as the Good Shepherd—one who would lead him through the experience of death as a shepherd leads his sheep through danger. Amelia considered it most fitting to hear the bleating of new lambs on the hillside during Josh's service.

The preacher also read a passage from the fourteenth chapter of the Gospel of John. "In my Father's house are many mansions: if it were not so, I would have told you. And if I go and prepare a place for you, I will come again, and receive you unto myself; that where I am, there ye may be also."

Amelia had no concept of what heaven would be like, but she knew that, by God's grace, Josh's heavenly dwelling would be superior to the one he'd left behind. Jesus had told His disciples that He would have a place prepared for them. Josh was now living in the presence of God.

Amelia cried with Mandy, who broke into tears when the casket was closed, and she saw Josh's face for the last time. The quartet sang slowly, "How beautiful heaven must be," as the casket was carried to the hillside grave. Mandy leaned heavily on the arm of her oldest son as the family filed along behind the casket.

Chase circled Amelia's waist with his arm, and she put her hand over his as they walked together. After the committal service, when they expressed their condolences to Mandy, Amelia told her that she was leaving in a few days.

"Oh, I'm going to miss you," Mandy said. "Come with me for a little walk."

"We shouldn't take you away from your family and friends," Amelia protested.

"I can see them often, but if you're going away,

I might not see you again. I want a few words with you.''

They all climbed to the spot where they'd picnicked a few weeks ago. ''Okay,'' Mandy said, ''let's have it! What's the matter with the two of you?''

''Mandy!'' Amelia said. ''We're all right now. Don't worry about us.''

''You two seem like my own young'uns, and I'm gonna talk to you like I would my own. Life is too short to deny what your heart wants. Though I lived with Josh over sixty years, the time passed fast. The two of you have got a heap of years yet, but the time will go faster than you think it will. Don't waste it.''

''Mandy, I'm ready,'' Chase said. ''I want to marry Amelia, but she doesn't want to make a mistake. She needs a little more time to be sure it's the thing to do.''

''The only mistake you've made was breaking up years ago.''

Chase looked quickly at Amelia.

''Yes, I told her,'' Amelia said. ''And also why.''

She turned her attention to Mandy. ''I was on the verge of saying 'yes' when we encountered the other woman a few days ago. I've forgiven her and Chase, but what if I'm never able to forget? Won't that be a problem in our marriage?''

''I don't suppose you will forget, but it won't

matter. I'm gonna tell you two something that no other livin' soul knows.'' She pointed to her family gathered below. ''You see my oldest girl down there? You've met her.''

''You mean Emily, the one who doesn't look like the rest of the family?'' Amelia asked.

''And for good reason,'' Mandy said. ''She ain't Josh's natural daughter.''

Amelia was too astonished to say anything, but she stared at Mandy.

''That's right. You know that Josh worked on the railroad, and he was gone weeks at a time. I was lonesome with only my little boy for company. I put up with it until Josh was transferred out West for six months, and I took up with one of the neighbors I'd walked out with before I married Josh.''

Chase saw the color fade from Amelia's face, and her dark eyes showed disbelief.

''I can't believe it,'' she whispered.

''It's the truth, though I ain't proud of it. When Josh came home, it was obvious I was going to have a baby, and it couldn't be his. I told him the truth, and he was awful mad, but because he loved me, he stayed with me. We left the little town where we lived in Kentucky, and we moved up here in this hollow, so nobody would know I'd been unfaithful.''

''And Josh didn't keep reminding you of it?'' Amelia said.

"Things were kinda strained for a while. Josh wouldn't touch me until after Emily was born, but he knew it wasn't Emily's fault, so he loved her like his own. They've always been close. None of our kids ever knew the difference. You know, Josh and me had a good marriage. He wouldn't have missed all of our years together because of one mistake on my part. I never strayed again. I'm trying to tell you, Amelia, that nobody is perfect. You're wasting time, fretting about the past, wasting days that you can't ever make up again."

Her throat tightened, and Amelia put her arms around Mandy. "Thank you," she whispered. "I don't know why I'm so hesitant. If Chase still wants to marry me, we'll get married right away."

"I still want you as my wife." When she turned from Mandy, he put his arm around her. "I always have."

As they walked down the mountainside, Amelia asked, "What will you do, Mandy? Will you go to live with one of your children?"

"Not as long as I'm able to take care of myself. I'll feel closer to Josh if I stay right here." She looked around the area, and an inner peace shone from her eyes. "These mountains hold a lot of memories for me. I'll be happier here than any other place." She smiled slightly. "My kids will kick up a fuss, but I'm stayin'."

Amelia hugged her again. "This is goodbye then.

Chase is going back to Ohio tonight, and I'll leave in two days for Philadelphia.''

"Then I won't see you again?"

"Oh, Lord willing, you won't get rid of us that easy. We'll come back to visit you," Chase said, "but I pray that it will be under more pleasant circumstances."

"I'm so sorry you've lost Josh," Amelia said.

"Don't grieve for him," Mandy said. "He went like he'd have wanted to. He hadn't had a sick day for years. He was in his rocking chair on the porch, and the Lord called him home. That's a good way to die."

Her gnarled hands patted Amelia's face. "The two of you have been such a blessin' to me. I'll be praying for you."

Amelia dabbed at her eyes, crying quietly as they walked out of the hollow. When they reached his truck, before he started the engine, Chase gathered her close.

"You're not supposed to grieve for Josh. Remember?"

Sniffing, Amelia said, "I'm not really grieving for him, but for Mandy who'll have to do without him. And maybe, a little bit for us—for the years we've missed being together."

"Don't fret about it anymore. Somehow, I feel that our new marriage will be even better because we were separated for a while. We'll never take each other for granted, because we'll know what we missed. The best is yet to come.''

They stopped for lunch, and over their Caesar salads, they discussed plans for the future.

''I think it's only right that I should be the one to move,'' Amelia said.

''And you don't mind?''

''Not at all. I'm sure I can find another position with the Red Cross in Columbus.''

''You don't have to work unless you want to,'' Chase said. ''My job pays well.''

''I probably won't at first. I'd like to spend a few months just being a wife.''

Chase's eyes were full of tenderness, but he teased. ''Will you have my meals ready, be standing at the door with my paper and slippers in hand when I come home every day?''

''Maybe so. But that wasn't *all* I had in mind,'' she said with a saucy wink.

''Now you're talking my language,'' he said, dropping a quick kiss on her lips as they left the restaurant.

When they returned to the truck, Chase reached into the glove compartment, took out a sheet of paper and gave it to Amelia.

''I received this e-mail from my mother. She asked me to pass it along to you, as she didn't know your address.''

Dear Amelia,

We saw your rescue of the child on the evening news. We hadn't realized that you were in the disaster area, but we knew Chase was, and we wondered if you were together. For several years we've wanted an opportunity to tell you that we're sorry for the breakup of your marriage. We know we weren't very good to you, and we've wondered how much that contributed to the trouble between you and Chase. He would never discuss it with us. Forgive us for not accepting you into the family. As the years passed, we've been aware of Chase's unhappiness. After seeing your daring rescue of the little girl, we realize even more that we should have appreciated you as a daughter-in-law.

Amelia sniffed again when she finished reading the letter. "So they won't object to another marriage?"

"Not at all, it seems. When can we get married, Amelia?"

"How about a month from today? That would be our mutual birthday, so we might as well have our wedding anniversary on the same date." With a grin, she added, "That would keep us from having to buy gifts for two different occasions."

"Sounds good to me," he agreed, amusement in his eyes.

"I'll return to Philadelphia, give notice to my supervisor, work two weeks, pack my things and ship them to your home. After I spend a few days with my parents, I'll come to you."

"My home is small, so we'll go house hunting as soon as we're married. Will we invite our families to the wedding?"

"Just our parents and your siblings. I'd rather keep it a quiet affair. Why don't you arrange a date with the pastor of your church? Vicky said you're good friends with her parents—maybe they could be our attendants."

"They will. You'll like them." He reached for her and she nestled in his arms. "I'll miss you, Amelia, but the time will pass quickly. After fifteen years, I can wait another month."

When they turned west on the highway, a sudden spring shower blew across the river from the southwest. It passed as quickly as it came, and the sun soon shone brightly. Dark thunderclouds on the western horizon were backlit by the sun, and a brilliant rainbow arched from one side of the Tug Fork Valley to the other.

"Oh, Chase, look! That means the rain is over. Our friends here won't have to face another flood. At least, that's the way it was when God created a rainbow of promise in Noah's time."

"That might be a sign for us, too. I believe God put that particular rainbow in the sky to show His blessing on our decision. At last, the storms in our lives are over."

"And we face the future together. I've always heard that love is sweeter the second time around. We'll soon find out," Amelia said. With a roguish gleam in her eye, she leaned toward Chase and nibbled his ear.

* * * * *

*Look for Irene Brand in a 2-in-1 book with
Dana Corbit, coming during the
2004 holiday season!*

Dear Reader,

By now, you've finished reading *Second Chance at Love*. Hopefully, you're cheering for Chase and Amelia and sharing the joy of their reconciliation.

During the writing of this book, my mind has often dwelt on God's willingness—indeed, eagerness—to give His people new opportunities to live abundant lives. Not only does He give the second chance, but the third, fourth, fifth—limitless opportunities for reconciliation with Him. No matter how many times we mess up our lives, His arm is outstretched to lift us from the mire of our mistakes. There is no problem so great that God cannot solve it.

Consider people in the Bible who have been favored with second chances—Adam and Eve, Noah, Abraham, Jacob, Samson, David, Peter and Paul. Although these people of faith are often remembered for their failures, we rejoice in knowing that they rose above their mistakes and took another opportunity to be faithful in God's service.

Whatever mistakes we've made, God is willing and able to give other chances to serve Him.

May God bless you.

Irene B. Brand

Love Inspired®

HERO IN HER HEART

BY

MARTA PERRY

Nolie Lang's farm, a haven for abandoned animals, gave hope to the disabled. Working with the injured firefighter Gabriel Flanaghan, who refused to depend on anyone, including God, tested her faith. Could Nolie make Gabe see that, no matter his injuries, he would always be a hero in her heart?

Don't miss

HERO IN HER HEART

On sale April 2004

Available at your favorite retail outlet.

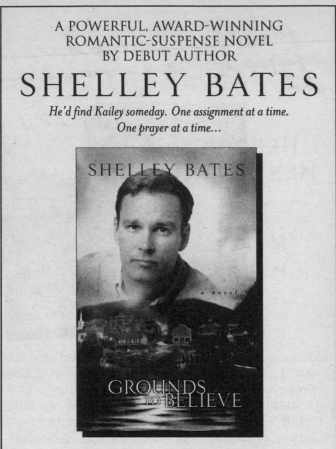

A SPELLBINDING HISTORICAL ROMANCE
BY INTERNATIONALLY ACCLAIMED AUTHOR

ROSANNE BITTNER

Against the rugged splendor of Alaska during the 1890s gold rush comes an inspiring love story and journey of discovery....

When Elizabeth Breckenridge is caught up in a difficult situation, she has no choice but to set sail for Alaska to live with her minister brother. On the long voyage, Elizabeth becomes increasingly drawn to Clint Brady, a cynical bounty hunter who shoots to kill. As traveling companions, they discover the awesome beauty of the Alaskan frontier, and their attraction to each other deepens. Can Clint let go of his notorious past long enough to see that heaven is no abstraction in the sky, but something they can experience together?

Love Inspired

LOVE IS PATIENT

BY

CAROLYNE AARSEN

There was more to Lisa Sterling than met the eye.
Dylan Matheson's new secretary was hiding
something—the reason why she was working for
him. Accompanying her boss to a family wedding
showed Lisa a softer side to the businessman. When
her secret was revealed, could God make Dylan see
that love was all things, including forgiveness?

Don't miss

LOVE IS PATIENT
On sale April 2004

Available at your favorite retail outlet.

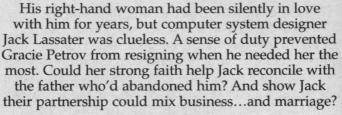